# ROBERT NEWTON PECK
# HORSE THIEF
A novel

**HARPERCOLLINS**PUBLISHERS

Horse Thief
Copyright © 2002 by Robert Newton Peck
All rights reserved. No part of this book may be used or reproduced
in any manner whatsoever without written permission except in the
case of brief quotations embodied in critical articles and reviews.
Printed in the United States of America. For information address
HarperCollins Children's Books, a division of HarperCollins
Publishers, 1350 Avenue of the Americas, New York, NY 10019.
www.harperchildrens.com

Library of Congress Cataloging-in-Publication Data
Peck, Robert Newton.
    Horse thief / by Robert Newton Peck.
        p.    cm.
    Summary: In 1938, with the help of a doctor and her elderly,
horse-thieving father, a seventeen-year-old orphan steals thirteen
horses from Chickalookee, Florida's doomed rodeo and finds a
family in the process.
    ISBN 0-06-623791-2 (alk. paper) — ISBN 0-06-623792-0 (lib.
bdg.)
    [1. Horse stealing—Fiction.   2. Rodeos—Fiction.   3. Horses—
Fiction.   4. Orphans—Fiction.   5. Florida—Fiction.]   I. Title.
PZ7.P339 Hq   2002                                    2001039733
[Fic]—dc21                                                  CIP
                                                              AC

Typography by Andrea Vandergrift
2   3   4   5   6   7   8   9   10
❖
First Edition

*To rodeo royalty:*
*Casey Tibbs, Larry Mahan,*
*Everett Shaw, Jim Shoulders,*
*and Miss Faye Blackstone.*
*They'll be revered and remembered*
*by one author*
*and the galloping ghosts of horses.*
*And also to Jaye Anders,*
*who can spin a rodeo rope*
*better than I can.*

*—R.N.P.*

# HORSE THIEF

# PROLOGUE

*Chickalookee, Florida*
*1938*

We was only a bunch of boys.

Yet with a biting ache to be *men*, as battered and bowlegged and brawly as the regular rodeo pokes that got bruised, got paid, got drunk. In that order.

Too often, some of the growed men earned little more than applause for the grit it took to silently swallow the bellowing pain of a busted bone. Boys earned a dollar a week and board, plus a bunkhouse cot with no springs. Standard wages for rural Mosquito County grunt labor.

Ah, but whenever a bevy of gigglesome gals sashayed to our arena for the weekly show, we'd slick pomade on our pompadours. You could smell us coming. We'd strut around in snug, ragged, washed-out jeans, deep denim blue now faded to a ghostly gray. Peekaboo kneecaps. Due north of the jean snaps, a few of us sported a fake-silver belt buckle that we'd buffed brighter than the chrome bumper on a fresh Ford.

For headgear, Tockerson's, a local feed-and-tack store, offered cheap cowboy-style haymaker hats of molded cardboard that traded for six bits. Seventy-five cents. If pampered, a haymaker might endure from early June to the final pant of August, when it will have melted into a soppy wet Kleenex.

Our work shirts had also tired to gray.

Dangling by a thread from a shirt flap was a small tab to tighten the drawstring of a pouch of cigarette tobacco. In a back pocket of our jeans nested a round, modest-size can of snuff, called dip. Or a Trojan that would probable remain as untried as its owner. Nonetheless, we viewed our swaggering selfs to be the slickest onions in the patch.

Some of us could even spit without drooling.

What we dudes smugly considered smarmy, in town at the Rusty Nail, was to round dance one-on-one with a gal, sweet-talk her, and smoke a roll-your-own. All to once. In time with the music, we'd attempt a head-on collision with her at every other step.

By 1938, our nation had stumbled into what folks sadly called the Great Depression. Jobs were scarcer than lawyers in heaven; thus we boys grunted at ours, seven days a week, choring rodeo stock that had to be well-fed to perform healthy. And rearranging the manure.

No one dared to quit.

Where would we go?

None of us had a home, as we were mostly orphans. Nobody mentioned a father. A few spoke of a mother, possible imaginary, who was off somewhere. For all of my years, people had called me Tullis Yoder. Yet if there be a Mr. or Mrs. Yoder, or kin, they certain kept distant. Upon escaping the orphanage at age nine (a guess), I'd lived with close to a dozen families that needed a farm-hand who'd sweat long hours and sleep in a barn. Lean wages and a leaky roof. I seldom said a so long as I went hitchhiking to the next misery. Perhaps what bonded us young bucks together was a common mistrust of our boss, Mr. Judah St. Jude. He was hobnail hard. Tall, lanky, lean as a dry-spell bean, he had a acidy nature. Meaner than a stepped-on snake.

One of the cowboys summed him up by allowing: "Instead of a sugar tit, ol' Judah got weaned on a pickle."

But, on Saturday afternoons, introducing himself over the loudspeaker, Judah would pronounce his own snooty name as though it was the most sacred word in the gospel. He was the official host and MC of the outfit we slaved for—not a genuine rodeo, which I itched to compete in, but a cow-and-horse show featuring broncs and bulls called . . . the Big Bubb Stampede.

Our chief brag: America's Biggest Cowboy! Not actual the main attraction. Merely its comic symbol. Big Bubb Nilbut was billed as weighing five hundred pounds. He rode a Clydesdale horse—Clyde—and in the arena, he bulldogged Oxford, a giant Holstein bull. Bubb was no cowboy, and Oxford was more of a bull-dog puppy than a bull. He was a ox that, to fool the crowd, displayed a false pair of spherical enthusiasms that had been attached in the rear by needle and thread.

Clyde and Oxford were, so to speak, both geldings.

Our Stampede crew claimed, in private, that Bubb fitted right in as a third, because our quarter-ton cow-boy's voice chirped higher than a chickadee. Bubb was forbidden by Judah to utter a word in public.

Wild Wes Winchester was our star. He looked, dressed, and acted like a silvery-haired Buffalo Bill and performed on horseback as a trick-shot expert with a pair of Colts. Wes could puncture a target behind his back, using a mirror. And break balloons with a long bullwhip. Or shorten, shorten, shorten a white soda straw clenched in the trusting teeth of our glamorous cowgirl cutie, Miss Thalia June Soobernaw. At the whip's final crack, however, us boys figured that Thalia June spatted out the last inch of straw. To tomfool tourists.

Judah called our paying crowd "the suckers."

That man never knew laughter. Even when he faked a smile, Judah's mouth was a scar that slashed across a foul face.

On the other hand, Wes Winchester was a solid Chickalookee citizen and more decent than any man ought. A daddy to us homeless boys with a winsome personality. At his act's finale, he'd gallop by the bandstand and blow a kiss to Ruby.

Ruby Red and her Saddle Tramps served as our all-girl brass band, but it'd been decades since Ruby was a girl. Beneath her flaming red wig, she had wispy white hair. Ruby was married to a no-count younger husband, Bix Bucko, our rope spinner. Her *boy toy*. She bought him fancy duds—shirts, boots, hats—and supplied him with liquor and Lucky Strikes.

It was always Wes who'd comfort the injured.

Or the sick of heart, such as poor Ruby whenever Bix latched on to some hot little buckle bunny and failed

4

to report home at night. Bix Bucko and Thalia June Soobernaw did riding and roping tricks together. And, rumor held, a few private performances.

It was all Wes could handle, keeping Ruby sober enough to toot her cornet.

Thalia June had winked at me more'n a few times. Although she sure was a whistle-at gal, I never took it too serious, as her arsenal of winks fired in all directions. In her skimpy little barrel racer skirt, mostly fringe, Thalia's tawny thighs deserved devout attention.

Thalia June Soobernaw was so talented a trick rider that Wes claimed she might become the next Faye Blackstone.

Hardly at all did I try to buddy the people I worked alongside. Boys never seemed to stay on the job very long. Come and go. It was the horses that held my heart. Once the bulls, bulldog steers, and roping calfs got tended to proper, I could fritter extra time on a portion of my job that was so rewardingly wonderful that it wasn't work.

It was worship.

I thought of each horse as mine, be it our ugliest bronc or Mr. Judah's white Arabian, Signature. I'd comb their tangled manes and tails, sponge off dirt, pick up every hoof to remove pesky little stones or glass. In warm weather, a thorough currying to remove tufts of underhair helped keep an animal cool. If trough water appeared muddy, it was a pleasure to bucket-fresh it. Every day, even during my time off, my hands stroked and patted each horse, feeling how they all knew me.

The horses were my family.

Matters abruptly changed. Some of our experienced

bronc busters got tired of living in one place, tired of the show business and its poor pay, and walked out on Mr. Judah St. Jude. Taking their saddles in order to hit a competitive rodeo circuit. Oh, how I longed to go with them and be a bull rider in a real rodeo.

Judah circled us all together for a talk-to, and then he played us like a deck of marked cards.

"You boys," he hacked at us between coughs, "are about to become rodeo *professionals*. At tomorrow's show, y'all git to fork some arena stock, in front a crowd. Broncs and bulls."

"Honest?" I asked in a doubting voice.

"Yup." His eyes narrowed at me. "You're to seek a future fortune at *my* expenses. No fee. It's a *re*-ward. Some'll you might git tossed and eat dirt, but tumbles are fun and they please the people." He paused to suck in a wheezy breath. "What's more, as a bonus, each a your names will be formal announced, by *me* personal, out over the speaker. You buds is about to *blossom*."

Hearing the news sprouted me a inch.

Trouble was, none of us had the brains or bowel to ask ol' Judah if'n we was to draw performance pay. The news itself was bigger than believing.

Wow! I'd be Tullis Yoder, one of the main arena talent. Could I wait until tomorrow's afternoon show? My innards was already doing somersaults as though attempting to digest a stump. But there was one power-ful punch that I never saw coming.

Gutbuster.

# CHAPTER 1

"Good luck, boy."

Too gut-fluttery even to mumble a thank you to the chute man, I forced a phony grin, stretching out a leg to straddle the massive back of a Galloway bull.

The brute felt hotter than a tent show sermon.

My mind kept repeating, *eight seconds*. That's how long a bulltopper has to stick his seat on bucking stock to win hisself a belt buckle. Until now, it had seemed a short time. But this wasn't a rodeo. I doubted that any buckle Mr. Judah St. Jude might award would be genuine silver. Or genuine anything.

"Thong your right hand snug tight," the chute man's partner said. "That's it. Take your time, on account this here animal ain't about to wander nowhere. Wrap the rawhide twice around. Wait up. As your hand's a mite puny, loop it three. Good. Pound the braiding into your glove palm and *squeeze*, like you'd sweet a gal."

He smiled with all eleven of his teeth.

"Anything else?" I asked him, hearing the bull snort and feeling his hoof pawing the turf.

"Pretend you're in a real rodeo. Keep a holding your left arm high up, above your shoulder, even though there ain't no judges here. Thataway nobody'll suspect you're turning soft or grabbing leather."

"A bulltopper," Chigger Dill, our lame and aging barrel clown, told me early this morning, "always remembers his first bull. And tries to forget his last." I had yet to attempt my first, but in a few more seconds, Gutbuster was mine to master.

Not knowing my exact age, or even my birthday date, I figured I'd turned seventeen. That made me older than Gutbuster and ought to mean wiser.

"If'n ya spill," the other guy advised, "git to your feet, even if your pants is down and both your legs is broke, and make for a fence. Some railbirds will be setting on it, creasing their butts, and they'll help fetch you up and over."

Beneath me stood a bull bigger than a boxcar. His temper rumbled like thunder. My stomach was fidgeting and my throat was too dry to swallow. My heart was a drum. The bull roared. Between my legs a hot rush of urine clouded my jeans a shade darker. One of the tenders noticed. Yet didn't poke fun.

"We all done it, sonny. Myself more'n once. I seed seasoned bullers wet theyselfs. Ain't no sign you're yeller. Just a human bean."

"Hey, look below," his helper said, pointing down. "That'n bull took hisself a pee. Poor curly head critter is possible a feared that you be aboard him."

Everybody laughed except me.

8

Eight seconds . . . only eight seconds.

"Y'all listen up," blared the arena loudspeaker with the squawking, familiar voice of our boss, Mr. Judah St. Jude. "Folks, di-rect your attention at gate number three. Tullis Yoder, one a our amatoor lads, fixing to make his virgin voyage . . . first rodeo appearance . . . on a bad bull named . . . Gutbuster!"

Tenders cinched the bite strap.

Under me, the bull flinched. A thick board near cracked. Behind, a third guy jabbed the bull's testicles with a electric prodder, to enrage him. I wanted to climb off. No, I wouldn't! My mind and spirit had been running too long, to escape who I was: a nobody. Best I quit turning tail.

Hands and fingers appeared as the chute crew prepared to swing open the gate. "Ya ready, Tullis? Say when."

A free hand tugged the cowboy haymaker snugger to my skull. My teeth gnawed each other. Nodding, I said, "Let'em rip."

As gate 3 pulled open, Ruby Red and the Saddle Tramps whacked into "Rattlesnake Rag." A furnace-hot hunk of male meat charged free, like flame, heated by hatred and pain. On the flank strap beneath his belly, a cowbell clanked like it'd gone crazy.

The gate didn't open clear enough. One of the latch boards tore at my knee, near wiping me clean off. Leaving the ground, Gutbuster's first jump took off north but landed south, swapping ends, punishing the earth with a jarring thud. He was a bass on a hook plug, his horns shook side to side. Hoofs again bit sand, driving the blade of his bare back into my crotch, and I'd got sliced to halfs, sending me sick into pain. My anus burned like arson.

"Eight!" I tried to holler, screaming, praying the bull would stop. "God . . . oh, God, shut him down. Please make him quit."

No brake on a rodeo bull. Neither reins nor saddle, and no thick lanyard rope attached to his nose ring. I'd seen Gutbuster dump a dozen cowhands. Why was I trying to top this cusser? Insane with ire, he broke air, hurting and twisting, spooked by the loudspeaker, crowd noise, and a persistent brass band, concentrating on the cause of his agony: a boy on his back.

Head low and heels high, he began to spin, and with us spun all of Florida. Trapped in a blur of whirling dust, frozen in fear, my body was mashed into madness. Boy and bull pain interlocked into a single torment. Twice a second, my neck and spine whip-snapped, like a snake being shook by a dog.

His twirl was too fast, his circling too tight to counter. Instead of leaning inside, my torso yanked out, my inside leg losing its hold. My hand couldn't pull me to him. Fury pounded my privates whenever his bucking would camel up.

Hurt worse when his hoofs hit.

Every part of me left him, save one—my right hand stuck, tightly thonged within the three braided-leather loops. I fell. Below him now, near his prancing hind quarters, my boot heels dragged in the gravel. I hung suspended by a entrapped arm, fingers warped by their impossible purchase on a bull's hump.

"Help . . ."

Suddenly seemed to be a horse nearby, and a shouting rider. Two horses. Pickuppers trying to sandwich a furious animal to release the bite strap, correct my tangled body, and free my hand. They couldn't still his bucking. A hoof hammered my ankle. Twice. Finally, hand tearing free, I fell onto the arena's sandy surface, turning, bouncing to a helpless heap.

Numb, I felt nothing. Saw nothing, as though I'd got dropped, at midnight, into some unknown ocean.

Then I knew that Chigger Dill and another rodeo clown were baiting the bull: "Hyah! Hyah! Heeyah!" I was hoping the sweeper crew could haze the brute away. Far away. Gutbuster, go 'way.

Lying flat, face in the dirt, I wondered which bones I busted, too afraid to stir. In shock, I stayed on my belly, inhaling and chewing the stink of dried manure, hidden in the shame of defeat, sensing the soil now sticking to my sweaty-wet face. Trying not to throw up. Or cry. My fingers clawed the ground.

Raising my head a inch or two, my eyes managed to blink through the dust and grit to check my damage. Gutbuster hung a helping of hurt on me. Squinting, it wasn't easy to accept the raw bleeding mess I saw at the end of my right arm.

Half a hand was gone.

# CHAPTER 2

W es Winchester pressed a rag to the bloody wound. A few minutes earlier, he and another man had slowly led Tullis, who could barely limp, to Wes's trailer. Even before the other fellow took leave, Wes had circled a short loop of twine around the lad's wrist to stem the bleeding.

"You'll clot," he told Tullis. "Youth heals quicksome."

After a minute or two, Wes cautiously loosened the clamping. "A too-tight tourniquet ain't a permanent fix," he said, eyeing the shiny, persistent flow of blood. "Your paw got tore up fearful. Our worst worry ain't that you'll die from blood loss. It's infection. So we'll allow your hand to drain a mite, to flush it out by Mother Nature's method."

"Thanks for the doctoring, Wes."

"Rest easy, son. All you lost was two littlest pinkie fingers. But you'll do passable with a pair of stumps."

The boy kept staring at his mangled right hand as though hypnotized. Tough, Wes thought, for a young'n

12

to cripple so early in life. But considering the heft of that Galloway terror, Gutbuster, maybe Tullis spilled off lucky. Even though he failed to stick for eight.

From inside the trailer, they heard the show continuing. Frequently there'd be Judah's voice on the speaker, heralding another horse or bull, followed by Ruby's frenzy of brass blowing. Today, that was almost always followed by a crowd's concerned moan. Wes understood why. Another beardless rider had gotten tossed. Or worse, trampled.

The day before, Wes had warned Judah about allowing inexperienced boys to fork bulls and broncs. Too risky. Fans wouldn't appreciate so much mayhem. Judah disagreed. What could Wes do? After all, the Stampede wasn't his to manage.

"Stay put," Wes ordered Tullis. "I got to mount up again to ride in the grand finale parade."

"Will you be back, Wes?"

Wes winked. "Soon as Ruby murders 'Dixie.'"

Outside, in the arena, the so-called Big Bubb Stampede stars were already in the saddle. There were also, Wes observed, a few busted-up chute attendants and stall muckers, in fresh shirts, who generally didn't appear to the public. Due to ample accidents, the parade was lean of personnel, so some extras had to be tapped, recruited to flesh out their fancy finish.

Bix Bucko, as usual, bore the American flag, Old Glory, as Thalia June Soobernaw flaunted the state flag of Florida. The ends of their short flagpoles neatly nested into tiny right-stirrup slots. Wild Wes Winchester made his grand entrance last, inspiring the entire audience to stand up and whoop a rebel yell for the proud Confederate banner, the red-white-and-blue Stars and Bars. On cue, the band whacked into "Dixie" like it had to be trapped, skinned, and gutted.

It was childish, Wes confessed, to enjoy such a boot out of receiving the loudest ovation. It always made him grin.

Wes watched as Judah flourished a final entrance on his white Arabian, Signature. Alongside him rode Big Bubb Nilbut on Clyde. Bubb and Judah doffed their white cowboy hats to salute the appreciative crowd. Bubb did his customary stunt. Selecting a little girl in a pink polka-dot dress, Bubb gave her a short, tight-circle ride, at a walk, cradling her aboard Clyde. As everyone laughed, Bubb quickly returned the smiling child to her proud yet slightly concerned parents.

The little girl kissed Bubb's cheek.

The band stopped its tooting. All was quiet. Expecting that the show was over, our tourist trade prepared to leave their folding-chair seats to head for home or hotel. What the public didn't anticipate was the most spectacular event of all.

The horses! Without any riders.

With the exception of bucking stock—three ornery outlaws—the Stampede's show horses were allowed to enter the empty arena, unsaddled and unbridled, to prance around in the open. All of them giddy. They seemed to know it was their time, to feel free and full of frolic. A horse revels in the company of other horses.

No malice. Only merriment as they nipped and nuzzled one another.

There was no band music. Instead, it was silent as a prayer.

As Wes quietly watched, Tullis unexpectedly appeared beside him. The two looked over the chin-high rails. "I don't guess," the young man said in a soft voice, "that I know a lick about heaven. But if'n there be such a place, it'll be a green meadow in a blue sky. And stocked with every breed of horse ever created. None'll be owned. No bits. No iron to bite on. Not one spur. Each horse will be liberty loose."

Wes swallowed. He rested a leathery hand on a lean, too-skinny shoulder. This boy could use a meal.

Or a home.

# CHAPTER 3

O.B. Swackert adjusted his new Stetson.

The mirror on the wall of his Chickalookee office, adjacent to the jail, was too skimpy for the sheriff to revere his entire reflection. Yet he could admire a hat, head, and beefy shoulders.

Quite a resplendent view.

With a satisfied smile, Odessa Bob cocked his head, admitting how dashing he appeared, for a man almost forty-nine. A spanker of a new cowboy hat, in a shade of pale silbelly, trimmed off a few years. Maybe even a few pounds. He wouldn't be a peace officer forever. Not with higher offices and more impressive titles for grabs. Smile widening, O. B.'s thick hand tipped the Stetson, as though practicing to greet a woman voter.

"Good morning, Miss Hibisca. What lovely weather we are enjoying, and that fetching frock you're wearing do look summery," he told the mirror. "How, pray tell, is your dear sister, Miss Elspeth? Feeling poorly? If so, I must stop around, of course with my Ulivia, and pay a call."

The sheriff once again touched the stainless brim, adding a courtly bow. "Mayor Odessa Bob Swackert."

My, how he rightly favored the sound of it.

Not always had he appreciated his full name. As a boy, he considered Odessa to be sort of girly. Growing up among the cow flats and canebrakes of Mosquito County, he cottoned to be called just plain Bob. Later on, however, he became aware that every Tom, Dick, or Harry was named Bob. Hardly a significant handle.

"Ah," he addressed the mirror, "but Senator Odessa Bob Swackert might someday ring like a church bell. Or resound in Tallahassee."

Reluctantly leaving the mirror, O. B. lectured himself to wear his church suit more often on weekdays. And buff his boots to a prosperous shine. As he looked out the window that faced Exchange Street, the sheriff felt the political smile slowly melt off his face and run down his shirtfront. Like spilled supper. Approaching his office door was somebody with a resolute purpose spurring her stride.

His wife, Ulivia.

Generally speaking, Miss Ulivia's so-called personality was dry ice. She was toast from stale bread, without jam or jingle. Ulivia, he gradually learned, didn't please. O. B. had tried. When they married, he'd even adopted her son, renaming the boy a Swackert. He shuddered. His stepson, Futrell Hoad Swackert, had the brains of a dung beetle. Nevertheless, O. B. had been pressured by Ulivia until he had appointed Futrell as his only deputy and pinned a star to his stepson's enormous shirt.

17

Easy done. Difficult to undo.

Hardest to bear was Futrell's calling him Papadaddy, a name that grated Odessa raw. It was especially upsetting when he called him that after adding another dent to their patrol car's fenders.

Odessa Bob held back cussing.

For sound reason. Ulivia was the daughter of a powerful politician who controlled most every voting Democrat in Mosquito County, making sure that a sufficient number of them voted twice.

E. Carvul Hoad, a Justice of the Peace, had no wife and no sons. Only one cherished daughter, Ulivia; perhaps the only citizen in the locality who could abide him. The Judge, as he was called, had hinted that Odessa, his son-in-law, might have a political future. Providing he avoided arresting the wrong people, who, The Judge made clear, were the *right* people.

O. B. sighed.

The Judge dealt out far more stick than carrot. Hard to say who was the Democratic Party's most pompous windbag: the late William Jennings Bryan or Elberton Carvul Hoad.

Ulivia exploded through the door.

"You," she said, leveling a finger at her husband, "best start budgeting to afford our Futrell a substantial pay raise."

"How come?"

"Because, if all goes well, he's fixing to get married." She held up a warning hand. "Not a word. I have it entirely arranged."

18

Who? O. B. couldn't immediately recall a face or a name. But what young lady in her right mind, O. B. mused, would ever consider marrying Futrell Swackert?

Ulivia beamed. "Her dear mother, Emolly Sue, and I have engineered the whole affair, and we are both pleased as punch. Believe me, this shall be a wedding to make Chickalookee society stand up and salute. Or bow."

"Aha." O. B. gulped. "The lucky miss is . . ."

"Clemsa Louise Wetmeadow."

# CHAPTER 4

H itch couldn't resist a chuckle.
    Knees bent, his bare feet braced on the outer edge of his jail cot, he leaned his spine against the cement wall of his cell. Listening and laughing. That woman had the voice of a wounded goose.

"Poor ol' O. B.," he muttered. "Ulivia's warble could strip varnish."

Generally speaking, Rubin Leviticus Hitchborn favored sheriffs as much as crotch itch. Yet Hitch considered Odessa Bob Swackert a friend. Behind the five-pointed star and the starched shirt, Hitch figured there dwelled a rather decent citizen. A regular Joe.

How many times, Hitch wondered, had he been confined here, a guest in the Chickalookee jailhouse? Over the decades, this had to be at least the seventh or eighth. He'd been in so many cells, and used so many phony names, that he could no longer keep count.

Over time, Hitch and Odessa had exchanged pleasantries, shared bits of news, stale stories, and sometimes a fresh joke. A lot more'n once, O. B. had opened a cell door, as well as his black fiddle case, and applied resin to his bow so the pair of them could make music. A duet. It was impossible for Hitch to disfavor a man who could make a violin sing and dance.

Hitch's hand checked his shirt pocket, feeling the small, familiar metallic bulge. His harmonica was still there.

Ulivia's sandpaper voice had modulated into a higher key, like an overtuned banjo string. Hitch guffawed. He'd enjoy telling Ulivia that her G-string was too tight. Or too loose! Whenever her blabbering took a breather, Hitch heard O. B.'s baritone rumble some obedient reply. Several of which, Hitch perceived, didn't seem to mesh into Ulivia's expectations.

"Rude," Hitch said, ashamed. How dismannerly to eavesdrop on a dialogue between a husband and wife. Hitch smiled. With Ulivia present, he guessed the chatter was more of a monologue.

Stretching his feet to the damp floor, Hitch rolled to his side, feeling the rough edge of a jailhouse mattress scratching his cheek.

Why not blow a tune?

But after wheezing out only a few plaintive notes, Hitchborn knew his spirit wasn't in a musical mood. With a resigned shrug, he returned the harmonica to its gray pocket. Shirt pockets were for carrying a man's most precious items: a harmonica, for one. In the other, a small photograph of his heart's dearest dream, Miss Faye Blackstone, which he took out to look at. Hitch could still see her on a horse; she was the most talented trick rider he'd ever seen. And prettier than honey on a waffle.

He didn't actual know Miss Blackstone personal. Only respected her from afar. She was a young gal and Hitch an old goat. With a sigh of longing, he tucked Faye's photo back into its safe-keeper pocket.

How long had he been here?

Hitch had been an invited visitor in too many facilities to total. They varied. But in every one there hung the same sullen smell; sour, done in. Even after release, he could inhale that particular stink of stale urine and wasted lives.

"Hey!"

A young voice in the next cell was calling out.

"Sir, if you're a horse," Hitch answered, "you're plumb out of luck. On account I am fresh out of *hay*."

The voice asked, "You got any smokes?"

"Nope. Do you?"

"I got Camels. But don't got no matches."

Feeling in his pants pockets, Hitch found nothing except seventeen cents. A dime, a nickel, and two coppers. No match.

"Hold on, sonny."

No bigger than a shoe box, the tiny barred window of his cell allowed little illumination from the outside. Compounding this, Hitchborn's failing eyesight. His age was seventy-seven beaten years. Curling back the cot's worn and fragrant mattress, Hitch ran his fingertips along the seams. Men who'd spent jail terms often passed the time by stashing a few small but useful objects in places where jailers rarely searched. His fingers stopped. Ah! There it was. A tiny knot informed him of where the mattress had been opened to receive a trinket or two, and then resewn. He felt stitches.

His teeth, not what they once were, bit the thread.

Inside the crumpled stuffing, Hitch located a bent bottle cap, four razor blades, a firecracker, five .22 cartridges, a bloodred shotgun shell (he guessed for a 20-gauge), pins, a six-inch spike . . . and seven kitchen matches. The kind you could strike with a thumbnail.

Approaching the bars at the wall that separated their cells, Hitch spoke in a low tone. "You have Camels, or so you claim. Well, we're in luck. I found us some fire."

"Okay, okay. What say we swap?"

"Well, maybe I just might agree to a trade. Except for one minor obstacle."

"What's the snag?"

Hitch grinned. "Trouble is, I prefer Chesterfield."

The younger prisoner spat out a dirty word. "Who in blazes do you think you are? President Hoover?"

Roosevelt had been sworn in since 1933, five years ago. The gink with the Camel supply was not only crude. Also uninformed. But who cared? Nobody's faultless, and a free smoke would be welcome.

"You win," Hitch said. "Now listen up. Extract a lengthy thread from your pants or shirt. If short, link two or three threads end to end, so it's as long as you be tall. Fashion a loop with a slip knot. Lay it flat next to a wall."

"For what?"

"Hold patient. Wait for a cockroach—there's a plenty in here—to step a hind leg in the loop. Then snare him. But do it *easy*! If you yank off its leg, the roach'll be useless. Be gentle. Next, tie a butt on the other end. Then try'n point the roach my way. It's only about a four-footer trip. I'll take the Camel and, with the help of the same insect, return you a match."

The young prisoner swore again. "You serious?"

"Control your ire. Son, if you listen you'll learn more than if you cuss," Hitch whispered. "If'n our cockroach buddy heads the wrong way, gently, *very gently*, rein him back, to redirect him."

Hitch waited, laughing, hearing the frustrated oathing next door.

"Dang you, mister," said the Camel owner. "This bug don't perform worth a purple spit. You can't learn no cockroach to run errands."

"Oh, but ya *can*," Hitch insisted. "And all you need is the secret."

"What secret?"

"First, ya gotta be smarter than the roach."

# CHAPTER 5

◆━◆━◆

"Where we bound for, Wes?" I asked.

The pair of us were walking away from the Big Bubb Stampede area and entering a clean section of Chickalookee that was mostly private houses. Small ones. A dog barked at us, a warning that rodeo rowdies were not too welcome among the respectables.

"To meet a lady," Wes answered. "A nice one."

"Why?"

"Hush patient, Tullis, and you'll discover."

Wes Winchester pivoted a pointed boot up a short walkway at a small sign. In spite of having attended not even one schoolhouse day, I was proud to be able to figure the letters.

> **Dr. A. M. Platt**
> **Vet & G.P.**

I balked to a halt. "No, not a doctor."

"Do come along," Wes prompted. "Please don't

25

demand spurs put to your ribs at every pace."

Up three steps was a small, front veranda with two green rocker chairs. Wicker. Before Wes could twist the door ringer, the door opened, and there stood a gray-haired woman in a long white smock. Around her neck hung a doo-funny.

Glancing first at Wes, then me, she said dryly, "So, we have another rodeo calamity that needs patching."

Wes respectfully took off his cowboy hat, nudging me to do likewise. "Doc, this here is Tullis Yoder. If I may, I'll offer you a cash dollar to mend him. Or whatever you charge."

"Come in, both of you."

"Can't stay," Wes said quickly. "You'll locate so many things ailing *me* that I'll expire before I can bolt." He shoved me through the door and placed a crumpled dollar bill on a wooden stand. "Thanks for redeeming him. Tullis be a winsome boy."

He left.

Closing her door to bar my escaping, Doc commented, "Wesley Winchester's a right kind gentleman. Our town needs more like him, and more capable women like Ethel Smertz." Doc was referring to the smart lady who handled the horse show's business affairs. Ushering me into a medical room full of silvery gadgets, she pointed at a narrow leather-topped table. "Sit," she ordered me, like I was a hound.

I sat.

"S'matter?" she asked me. "What's busted?"

Pulling my right hand out of my pocket, I displayed

what was left of it. She winced. "At least you kept more'n half. Two fingers and a thumb. How'd it happen?"

"Bull." I was too shame-faced to say more.

"Did you stick?"

"No, ma'am. Gutbuster got rid of me."

"And took two of your pinkies for souvenirs." She sighed. "Let me examine. No! Don't pull away. I sound crabby, but I haven't bit anyone since noon." With my hand beneath a light, she asked, "When? Saturday? Two days ago?"

"Yes'm."

"You're open and raw. Ignore it, and you'll possible lose the whole shebang by infection. And folks'll call you Lefty." Piercing blue eyes bored holes in me. "Are you going to snivel? Don't. Just say that you trust me to tend you proper."

"I do. What's the geegaw around your neck?"

"Stethoscope." Taking it off, she plugged both my ears with black tips, pressing a silver cone through my ripped shirt and against my chest. It felt cool. "Hear the *thump-thump*? That's your heart. A gal will make it beat faster."

I smiled at her. "Yes'm."

"Tullis, is it?"

"Far as I know. Ain't got parents. Since recalling, I been Tullis Yoder. Other than a name, I'm nobody. A orphan."

Uncorking a bottle of colorless liquid that had a strange stink, Doc said, "This is alcohol. It'll sting you worse'n a hundred hornets." I retreated my hand a inch.

"If you're a bulltopper, or some other variety of fool, you best accustom your Mr. Nobody self to a short life of constant discomfort. Or a cheap coffin."

Doc swabbed my hand. She'd been accurate about the hornets, except they numbered over a hundred, plus a few relatives, cousins, and other assorted kin. While I howled and hopped around, calling the alcohol bottle a few salty names, Doc disappeared. Then she returned with a tumbler of creamy drink that I cogitated was probable her secret brand of poison.

"Drink up."

"What's it called?"

"Buttermilk. S'pose it sounds too goody-goody to a two-fisted Saturday night booze-puker such as your worldly self. But it'll help hasten your healing. If you're *my* patient, you march to my fife and drum. Either that, or you're discharged to limp your merry way and eventual smell your hand rotting off with the stench of a dead skunk."

"I never heard a no *lady* doctor."

"Is that right?" From a drawer in a white metal cabinet, Doc produced a spool of white thread, plus a needle that she baptized in alcohol. "Well now, sonny—I never heard of Tullis Yoder. Nor will anyone else if you allow infection to butcher you." Her voice lowered. "I've mended many a Florida rodeo star."

"Such as . . ."

"Grover Mills, Oz Freemont, Jack Dee, Tindly J. Shearman, to name a few. If you're in a mood to be impressed, also none other than Kicker Zell himself."

"You done doctoring on *Kicker Zell*?"

She snugged the first stitch into me. "Correct. After I finish lacing you up with my fancy embroidery, I might escort you next door, to meet Kicker. In person."

"Ouch! . . . You serious, ma'am?" She sneaked in another stitch. "We can actual meet Mr. Zell? Golly Joe Mary! Why, he's *famous*! Most celebrated bull rider that ever rid. Years and years ago, Kicker Zell was Florida State Champeen."

Another stitch. Dang her needle. Yet it made me forget the swarm of hornets. Kicker Zell! It was beyond breathing.

"Final one," Doc said. "You're some gutsy. I understand how it hurts. Please do not imagine I don't care. I do. Besides, you remind me of someone I once knew. Long ago."

"Who?"

Doc shook her head. "A boy with your brand of freckles."

After she encircled my hand with strips of clean cloth, tying me into a pretty Christmas package, we went next door and met Kicker Zell. He lived there with his older sister.

What a shock.

No longer a star-spangled rodeo star, the gent Doc introduced me to turned out pitiful sorry. A beat-up mess of a man, busted knuckles, half a mashed nose, and only one large nostril. Stitch tracks across his cheek all the way to a missing ear. A milky eye. Mr. Zell didn't speak. All he could do, according to his sister, was sit in a kitchen chair and stare out a window. I wanted to shake his hand, but he didn't know we was there.

On our way back to Doctor Platt's place, I asked her, "What's the age of that poor ol' duffer?"

"He is thirty-one."

"Is that all?"

"You just met a person whose body is mostly held together by screws, thread, and tape. He has been speechless since he was seriously throwed off and gored by a bull when he was twenty-four. Never spoken another word. His sister Evelyn has to feed him, wash him, put him to bed. He whimpers most of the night. Kicker doesn't even remember her name. Or his own."

Prior to taking leave of Doc, I thanked her. Also, in a polite way, I asked her how come she bothered to take me to meet Mr. Zell.

"So, that *you*, Mr. Nobody Bull Rider, could take a close squint at Kicker and view your own possible future."

# CHAPTER 6

"Here ya go, Bubb," I said, handing our oversized personality another big tumbler of cold water.

It was uncomfortable hot in Big Bubb's dinky trailer, even though I'd made sure to open both windows as far as possible, for a cross breeze.

Due to the bandage decorating the remainder of my right hand, I was no longer useful with raking the arena, dispensing hay or straw bedding, or unloading feed bags off a supply wagon. So Mr. Judah assigned me to assist all five hundred pounds of America's Biggest Cowboy.

"Thanks, kid," Bubb said in his little girl voice.

Repeatedly, I'd told him my name: Tullis Yoder. But it didn't register. Nobody at the Stampede credited Bubb with the brain of a chokecherry pit. They made sport of Bubb to his face and behind his back. Being his personal assistant was the absolute lowest job in our outfit.

It was a lot of heaving work.

Bubb Nilbut had to be helped to sit up in bed, to stand, and to walk. I brung him his meals and cleaned up his messes. All kinds. He was enormous but feeble.

Flab. No muscle. Like a good many hefty people, Bubb had a baby's face. Fat and funny. To the public, Bubb had a way of appearing happy, even though inside he was blue-hearted. Not so much, though, that he failed to ask me if my wrapped-up hand was painful. Told him it was.

"I'm sorry," he told me. "Hope it gets better."

Except for Miss Ethel Smertz, the nice woman who stopped in every day to see if Bubb needed anything, nobody came to visit Bubb. He didn't have one single sidekick. No buddies to get drunk with, to shoot eight ball with at the pool parlor, or to deal out a hand of stud poker to. Not even blackjack. Guys who'd known him a long spell claimed that poor Bubb had never enjoyed hisself a gal friend.

Oh, well, I didn't have a gal either.

To eye Bubb in his trailer, wearing his ratty old nightshirt that I hand washed, was enough to break my heart. He was a quarter-ton loser.

So I decided to be Bubb's friend.

He seemed to sudden sense my dedication. One time, when we were eating bacon, eggs, and grits together, Bubb looked at me and used my front name for the first time. "Tullis, you'n me, we certain be a pair of pokes, ain't we? I weigh five hundred, and you're a splinter."

"True," I agreed. "Me, always been gawky. My legs are skinny enough to get used as firm-joint calipers. Even though I got a appetite that could chew up a camel." Hoping not to sound unmannerish, I asked, "You always been fatsome?"

"Always. When I was a chubby kid, the meanies

called me Hoare Hog. Because my legal name is Nilbut Hoare. When I growed up big, and bigger, my folks never took me nowheres. On account they was ashamed that I looked like a pig."

"Did you leave home?"

"Had to. My mama died. Pop used to beat on me with his razor strap. Lock me inside my room for days without no food. So I run away. Only job open to me was being in a circus. A sideshow freak. That's where Mr. Judah spotted me and offered to make me a rodeo star."

"And you certain be one," I said, wiping some food stain off his chin and helping to slide his mighty arm into a sleeve of his shimmery black-and-silver show shirt. Special made.

"Naw." He shook his head. "I'm still a freak." He stared at me. "You understand. I never tell the others what I tolt you. Because you ain't mean."

"I'm going to be your friend, Bubb. Honest am."

"Thank you. And I'll be your friend, Tullis. How is that ol' hand of yours keeping?"

"Mending. It'll knit. Ya know, Bubb, it's been a week since the bull stomped me, but the hurting won't abate. Strange, but them two fingers I lost still ache."

As I awkwardly snapped Bubb's shirtfront together and added his fancy mother-of-pearl bolo tie, he looked down at his shirt, then up. His pudgy face turned frosty. And frightened. He asked, "Is today Saturday?"

"Yup. Show day. Hear the crowd? They're all filling the seats to see *you*, Bubb. To witness you riding into the arena, on Clyde, and applaud as you rope or bulldog

33

Oxford. That's how come they'll all clap and cheer." My hand whacked his shoulder. "Because you're a genuine *star*."

Lying to Bubb almost made me weep. He wasn't a real cowboy any more than our horse show was a real rodeo. To the audience, he probable wasn't even a person. Only a big blob of boffo.

He spoke in his squeaky mouse voice.

"Tullis . . . I'm afraid."

Those were the last words that my big buddy ever spoke to me. I wondered how he knew what was going to happen on that awful Saturday afternoon.

Like always, as America's Biggest Cowboy was fixing to make his entrance, our brass band was blasting out "That's a Plenty" in a minor key when chute gate swung open. One of the pokes prodded some sharp electricity into Oxford's rump, enough to force the ox into a trot. Pursuing him come Bubb on his hairy-hoofed Clydesdale charger. Bubb's customary arena stunt was to loop a rope around Oxford's neck or a horn. But Mr. Judah had told Bubb that roping wasn't a crowd pleaser.

Judah wanted bulldogging.

So, on this Saturday, instead of roping his ox, Bubb leaned out of the saddle to fetch a purchase around Oxford's blunted horns. He'd rehearsed this trick a few times, but not enough.

His arm missed hooking around the far horn. His balance lost, Bubb tried to right himself but couldn't. Falling off Clyde, he landed with a thunderous thump, rolling beneath both Oxford and Clyde. A big ox and then a big horse crushed the body of America's Biggest Cowboy. In the dust, the two beasts regained their footing, looking confused. But the bulldogger lay motionless. The crowd let out a long moan of concern, one final ovation that Bubb never heard.

His neck had snapped.

On the bandstand, one by one the brass instruments of Ruby Red's Saddle Tramps ceased, then silence. Hundreds of people could not speak. Except one—a baby cried. As I watched, my mouth opening in stunned disbelief, the child's crying seemed to echo another tortured childhood of long ago. Before I was born.

The tears of a young, tormented Nilbut Hoare.

# CHAPTER 7

Judah swore—nothing fancy, just a string of old favorites—spilling a glass of his best bourbon on the fly of his trousers. Seated in shade, on his comfortable throne in the announcer's booth near an electric fan, the MC eyed Bubb's lifeless body as it lay on the arena sand. Hurriedly, he signaled Ruby Red to get the Saddle Tramps going again, as if Bubb's dying was part of the program.

Over the loudspeaker, he drawled, "Folks, nothing's went wrong. So y'all please stay seated and permit our talented girlie band to entertain you."

"Toot Toot Tootsie" obediently blared at full blast.

Too late. An audience, largely comprising children whose parents had just been startled by Judah's careless, full-volume broadcast of profanity, preferred their off-spring not to hear more oathing, or see more dying. Seat after seat was rapidly being vacated.

"Now, next Saturday," Judah St. Jude pleaded in faked joy, "we'll present a extraspecial show. Right now, our sales booth is reopening, and the extravaganza tickets go on sale at a half-price bargain."

No use. Rows were emptying. Somebody remarked that Ethel Smertz had already closed the ticket counter and had driven away.

As a crew came running into the arena to examine Bubb and to quiet the two animals, Judah faced a bitter truth: the Big Bubb Stampede no longer had a Big Bubb, or much else. Doubtful he could locate another fat cowboy freak. In addition, his most talented riders and ropers had already abandoned him. The livestock was aging. Judah felt the sudden wrenching reality of being both old and shoe-hole broke. Ignoring Bubb's condition, Judah left the booth and rushed directly to his boardinghouse room where he changed from his sparkling rodeo costume into a gray business suit. Plus a serious tie. Then prayed his Caddy convertible would start.

The automobile was Judah's pride and personality. Above the grill, a long set of steer horns went winging as if in flight. The seats were upholstered in black-and-white Holstein cowhide. Most attention getting of all was the Cadillac's warning device that honked like the sawing hee-haw of a Florida mule.

"I still got style," Judah St. Jude said.

Slowly rolling into town, cautiously, to prevent his Stetson from blowing off, he parked beside the Mosquito County courthouse. Although near to three o'clock on a Saturday afternoon, he presumed the Justice of the Peace might still be in his spacious second-floor office.

He was. The door was open.

As though he hadn't heard Judah's timid knock, Judge E. Carvul Hoad didn't glance up from the papers on his expansive desk. Judah considered knocking again, or just sauntering inside. He did neither, waiting submissively in the hallway with his Stetson off until beady eyes squinted over half-moon glasses to appraise the visitor and evaluate his level of importance. Or usefulness.

Residents of Chickalookee presumed that Mr. Judah St. Jude owned the Stampede. Judah owned only a tenth of it, a modest slice of ownership that the Chickalookee National Bank would surely challenge. The remaining lion's share, ninety percent, belonged to Elberton Carvul Hoad, as did a plethora of other businesses, among them a seedy, edge-of-town enterprise that offered horizontal diversions, including a bar and billiards.

The Judge took his time in removing his glasses, wiping the lenses, and slowly hooking them over his protruding ears.

"I just heard," he snorted.

Judah wasn't surprised. In Mosquito County, little happened that didn't reach The Judge's ear. His informants were legion. It profited to stay on The Judge's good side, assuming he had one, as the bread at many a table was buttered by Hoad.

"I hear Fat Boy crashed and burned." The Judge cackled a laugh. "You plan to repaint the advertisement banner to read: 'America's Deadest Cowboy'?"

Judah, now standing with hat in hand, was not about to enter the office until invited. Judge Hoad, in his shirt-

38

sleeves and black arm garters, seemed to enjoy watching him squirm. "Who told Your Honor the news?"

"Ethel. Who else? As you know, every Saturday when the Stampede ticket booth closes, she brings me the cash box. It's already tallied and in my safe. A functional woman, Ethel Smertz. Keeps a eye on the loot and another eye on you." The Judge again amused himself with his own shrewdity.

"We ought to talk, Judge."

"No need. The show's over, Judah. It makes less and less money every week. Big Boob was the only oddity that made the attraction unique to the suckers. And now he's colder than a clam."

"What'll I do?" Judah St. Jude felt a gnawing horror weakening his speech. His hands sweated.

"Pack," The Judge snapped.

"Beg pardon?"

"Pack up'n git. Hightail out of town before the bank forecloses on your debts and that fancy jackass mobile you call a car. I just got off the contraption. Talked long distance to T. C. Threadgill, up in Fort Dee, who made me a offer to buy the livestock: bulls, broncs, roping calfs, plus the show horses. If they're still alive. No use trying to auction'em. Those ancient nags ain't worth the iron on their hoofs. T. C. will process every head. Grind'em up into dog food."

"Do I git a taste of the take?"

Judge Hoad tossed back a howl.

"You? St. Jude, you're into me for over a thousand smackers. No way to pay it back. But, I shall forgive the debt, providing"—he pointed a finger at Judah's crotch—"in writing you formally dismiss all employees. Except for Ethel. I got personal plans for her brains. If'n they refuse to vacate, warn'em that my son-in-law, Sheriff Odessa Bob Swackert, will clink'em into the slammer. For trespassing on my fee simple absolute."

Nervously shifting his weight to the other boot, Judah risked advancing half a foot or so inside the office. "Might be trouble, Judge. Over years, a few of my remaining hands formed sort of a attachment about them horses. Some vengeful punk could organize a backlash. Or burn our entire place down to ashes."

With a smirk, The Judge stood up.

"Fine with me if she burns. In value, the buildings and bleachers don't equal a cold winter squat. Besides, I already got a realtor's bid on the property. As to the horseflesh, be sly." His Honor winked. "Inform your young manure movers that you made a humane arrangement for the horses to retire to meadow." His eyes narrowed. "To be used for a children's church camp."

Absorbing how slippery The Judge could cut a deal, Judah had to credit the old geezer. Mosquito County's wealthiest citizen. Judah could easy see why.

Hoad milked people into goats.

# Chapter 8

——◆——

It hurt to bend his spine.

Chigger Dill was sorting through a lifetime's collection of gear and articles. He grunted. "Had it to do over, I'd half this stuff into two boxes. I'd label'em, 'junk not worth saving' and 'stuff too wore-out to save.'"

Until yesterday, his so-called treasure pile had been sheltered inside the bunkhouse, neighborly to his cot. But Judah had sudden cut off the electric juice, right after breaking the news that the glory years of the Stampede were now disperpetuated. Washed up for good. The hands had bagged their belongings and took leave. He figured the youngsters had also fled, without as much as a wave. Moving on to the next busted bone or soup kitchen. Chig would be the last member of the crew to cut out.

Because his eyesight was shot, Chigger had dragged his box outside into the late afternoon daylight. A crate full of memories. Piece by piece, he'd have to pitch away his life.

One souvenir wasn't in the box.

White Trash was a gray gelding that, years ago, had bucked him so high into the atmosphere that he near starved to death on the way down. Worse, the sombee kicked his kneecap. *Pop!* He'd heared it explode. Trouble with bronc or bull riding is that it's both discomfortable and short. White Trash had terminated Chigger's competitioning.

Switched to clowning.

Over a dozen years ago, Doc Platt had rescued his leg; for what, he still was unsure. Every step gritted his teeth.

Straightening up, Chigger shot a look over his shoulder at the horse corral. There was that youngster again, conversationing a mare. The kid with a bandaged hand who use to tend to Bubb.

With a smile and a wave, the lad called, "You still abiding, Chig?"

As the boy walked toward him, Chigger recalled his name. Tullis. That was it. A heck of a decent kid who didn't mix much with the other no-gooders. Stayed away from the pool hall and the crap games. Good worker. Actual made himself a friend to Bubb, and Big Bubb didn't boast many. In fact, Tullis might've been his only.

"Son, where you fixing to locate work?"

Tullis shrugged his bony shoulders. "No idea. Don't guess it'll be a lead-pipe cinch to find a job with a cripple paw." As proof, he indicated the bandage.

"S'pose not." Chig stuffed a porous pair of socks, one blue and one brown, into his duffler. "Hope you got family somewhere, so's you can bunk until ya knit. If'n

I could spare any change, I'd spring for a supper at the diner."

The boy sighed. "Ain't had a meal all day. Early this morning, I tried the diner, like usual. But no luck. The short short-order guy, Mr. Copeland, said he'd received notice not to feed us Stampeders our two-a-day no more." Tullis looked at the corral. "At least the horses were fed. A truck come with horse chow. On the cab, it said T. C. Threadgill Company. And underneath, Animal Food. I reckon that means hay or oats."

Chigger choked back his breathing.

Tullis didn't know!

Nor did Chigger have the heart to truth him. The Threadgill operation bought up stock mainly for one purpose: to butcher it into pet food.

Morning after morning, Chigger had noticed Tullis visiting the horse stock. Tending to their needs and talking personal to every animal. Touching them. The boy often pressed his face to a soft muzzle.

Best he change the subject. "Cousin of mine got a tree-and-plant nursery, south of Hallapoosa. Provided I can hitchhike that far, Ducoste will afford me a grunt job." Unable to resist, he glanced again at the horses. "Golly, I'm to miss rodeoing. The aroma of all them big animals."

"Wes and Miss Ethel always said you were a good barrel clown, Chigger. The guys agree, you helped to spook off Gutbuster when he was fixing to divide me into sections."

"Glad I survived you."

Tullis smiled softly. "I'm equal glad that Mr. Threadgill, or whoever they be, are going to save our horses. And find'em a meadow."

Chigger winced.

Chig wasn't what you'd call a churchgoer. However, he fervent prayed that this here decent kid would never learn about his beloved four-footers being converted into a snack for Tabby and Rover.

He wanted to give Tullis a special thing, a present that might cheer him a mite. Glancing into his junk box, he saw it all wadded up, worthless, and probable in need of washing. His rodeo clown costume. Wrinkled. The rainbow colors had faded to misty hues. Nonetheless, the clown suit might be fun duds a boy could cotton to.

"Ain't much," Chigger said. "But yourn if you want-'em." He handed the two-piecer to Tullis. Plus a wig and a hat.

"For me?"

Chig nodded. "Because I'm retired."

"Wow. Thanks a whole lot, Chig."

"Enjoy it, boy." He paused. "I suspect you been bit by the bug. It's a pox. Wanting to eight-second a bull is like a scab a feller keeps picking. Be a waste of good air to try'n argue you otherwise. But seeing as you're already chopped up, try clowning. You'll remain a lot handsomer with a barrel instead a Brahma."

"Even if I don't do any clown work, I'll always keep it, Chigger. I honest will." Tullis smiled. "Either way, I'll try to keep what's left of me unified."

"You do that."

Looking to his left, Chigger recognized an approaching person. She had pieced him back together. Three times. She was hurrying toward them as if completing a mission.

"Doc Platt," he said. "What's the rush?"

Stopping, catching her breath, the woman told them, "I heard the news about the Stampede's last whoop. Saw the CLOSED sign outside. And I'm sorry." Her voice softened. "Believe it or not, Chigger Dill, I'm going to regret not seeing you, Wes, Ruby. I'll sorely miss every one of you torn-up rascals. So I hastened here to say good-bye."

"So long, Doc," Chigger said. "I'm true grateful for all you done—every splint and every stitch of sewing."

"Likewise," Tullis added. "Thank you, ma'am."

"*You*"—Doc turned to face Tullis—"aren't leaving. If I can convince you to stay, young man, you're coming to live under my roof, in my care. I can't yet explain the reason."

Chigger cracked a easy grin. He reckoned why. Doc Platt's long-ago loss just might blossom into Tullis Yoder's gain. With one last polite nod to Doc, Chig walked away, hurting, but doing his proud best not to limp.

# CHAPTER 9

Clemsa Lou stamped her foot. Not a large foot, as Clemsa Louise's shoe size was a petite five, double A. Yet firmly put down.

"No." *Stamp. Stamp.* "Mama, darlin', with due respect to you and Daddy, I'm *not* fixing to become Mrs. Futrell Hoad Swackert."

With pink-flowered garden gloves and snippers, her mother divided her concern between a wandering jasmine and her daughter. "But Futrell is such a catch. And so polite."

Hauling the debris barrel closer, Clemsa yanked up a patch of pigweed with a bit more force than necessary. "Very polite. And about as exciting as opening night at a E-Z Car Wash." Clemsa added a broadleaf infestation to the barrel. "However, if I yen for manners, I'll curl up in bed with our Miss Emily Post etiquette manual."

"Clemsa Louise Wetmeadow!" Her mother covered her ears. "*What* would the Swackerts *think* if they could overhear you carry *on*?"

Unwinding several strands of wild pumpkin vine

from a bird of paradise plant, Clemsa said, "Mother mine, most every evening at our dinner table, Daddy and I hear *everything* that Ulivia Swackert *thinks*. And *says*. You repeat it like a Bible reading."

In frustration, her mother clip-clip-clipped her trimmers. "I can't *believe* I'm listening such from the mouth of my own offspring, who, if I may remind her, received her raising in a Christian household."

"Yes, Mama. And I am truly beholden."

Clemsa Lou moved closer to lop away a few dried pricker stubs from a thorny rosebush.

Her mother's glove tenderly touched hers. "I *do* hope you haven't forgotten that Futrell's granddaddy just *happens* to be Judge Elberton Carvul Hoad, who is Miss Ulivia's father."

Forgotten? Clemsa Louise had heard it, heard it, heard it, even in her sleep. Her mother's favorite tune. A broken record on the Victrola. Lifting some scattered leaves, she said, "Mama, I also know Futrell's real daddy was neither a Swackert nor a Hoad. His name was Dermitt. Folks called him Ditch Dermitt because whenever he slurped a jug of moon, which was weekly, a *ditch* was where he was usual found."

Her mother's hand slapped the barrel rim. "Where, I do wonder *where*, has your gentility *gone*?"

"Please stop, Mama. Your social ideal, Miss Ulivia, married early and unwisely. Result? A tipsy first husband and a simple son."

"I'm quite aware that your suitor isn't a replica of Mr. Thomas Alva Edison." She stepped closer to her daughter. "But darlin', this is your *chance*, your opportunity to marry The Judge's only grandson." She whispered, "To wed *quality*."

"And quantity."

"What *do* you mean, child?"

"Little ol' Futrell is sweet enough. But recent, on the weighing scales at Conron's Drug Store, the needle stopped shuddering at 245. It isn't all mentality."

Removing a glove, Emolly Sue Wetmeadow blotted her dampening palm with a delicate handkerchief. "But he *adores* you, precious."

Clemsa nodded. "Probable because Miss Ulivia so ordered. In that family, there is only one pair of pants, and not either Odessa Bob or Futrell pull'em up over their rumps."

Her mother gasped. "You have become so . . . so . . ."

"Outspoken?"

"Crudely outspoken."

"At the risk of shocking you, dear Mother, I am doing my darndest to *avoid* having *outspoken* Ulivia for a mother-in-law. I'd be trapped in a suggestion box. Add to that, Futrell actual told me that Miss Ulivia has the temper of a wet cat."

"I declare."

"So does your daughter. Respectfully, I declare *not* to become Mrs. Deputy Swackert, even though his stepdaddy, Odessa Bob, is a sweet ol' charmer. Futrell isn't nasty, Mama. He's plenty fine. So he deserves a bride who gazes at him like he's butter on a biscuit."

Her mother sighed. "Well," she responded at last, "if

you let Futrell slip through our fingers, whom *will* you marry?"

Troweling up a clump of goose grass, Clemsa said, "Mama, I realize you and Miss Ulivia have made plans. But I'm only *seventeen* and certainly *not* pregnant. So please don't needle Daddy to gallop me down a church aisle. To answer your question, I want a boy with *violins* in him. Poems. Rainbows and sunsets and meadow-larks."

"Clemsa Louise, you *mystify* me. Truly do."

"I'll explain." She touched both of her mother's shoulders. "Instead of Futrell's constant store-bought bouquets from the florist, I want a barefoot boy to pick me one yellow dandelion, with his toes, and then shyly present it to my hand."

"And what would *that* mean?"

Clemsa smiled. "For me, an entire garden."

Two women, who imagined that they understood each other so thoroughly, exchanged a mutual glance of affection. But again, the mother sighed.

"Oh, dear . . . how shall I face Ulivia?"

# CHAPTER 10

"Are you hungry, Tullis? I hope so."

After being asked to employ the Octagon to soap my hands at the sink, I was seated in a hard kitchen chair, admiring how rabbity Doc A. M. Platt could move at her stove.

"Yes'm."

Four pots bubbled like a steam engine. Each teased a aroma that my empty belly could slice and slip between bits of bread. I couldn't wait to work a fork. I sat patient in Doc's clean kitchen, inhaling cookery, hungrier than a woodpecker in a ironworks.

"You look skinny dreadful, Tullis." Doc Platt gave me a hurried look, up and down. "You're thinner than a bee's neck."

"Yes'm." With a grin, I said, "But perching here, a body could about gain a pound by just breathing."

The meal was worth the waiting. Brisket of beef, boiled little red potatoes under mushroom gravy, orange strips of raw carrot and bits of green pepper, onion slices, some cold cabbage shreds that Doc called slaw. Hot rolls with tiny black seeds that stuck between my teeth. Honey butter. Squash with yellow chunks in it that Doc said was pineapple. Doc didn't eat hardly a nibble. While I was shoveling it all in with both hands, she sat direct across the kitchen table, studying me.

Her voice smiled. "Save space for dessert."

"Ma'am, it better be a jelly bean, on account I'm so deep loaded. Thank you. Thank you much." As I sleeved off my mouth, Doc tossed me a napkin. "If there's outside chore work that needs, I'll tackle it."

"I could use a live-in helper here, Tullis. So you're welcome to stay a spell."

Before I could answer, Doc jumped up, disappeared into the booth pantry, and returned with a slab of pie that you could wedge under a barn door to hold it open. As I was putting myself outside it, I commented that her cooking was even more tasty than Mr. Copeland's diner's blue plate.

Doc bowed. "My, what an honor."

Together we did dishes. Doc washed. I dried.

"You sure got a tidy house. Do you live here by your lonesome?"

"I do now. My husband, Frank Platt, was a house-painter. Until a ladder slip cracked his spine." She paused. "A year earlier, we lost our only child. A son. His name was Hollis. He was fifteen, working under a Buick. A jack slipped and the car's weight crushed him." Doc smiled. "His face had freckles, like yours. Same blue eyes." She paused. "The day Wes brought you here and said your name was Tullis, it was quite a jolt. I felt as though you'd been sent to me by Divine Providence."

I was toweling off a cook fork. "Ma'am, where does this go?"

She pointed a soapy hand. "In that drawer."

Tucking the fork into its slot, I closed the drawer. "I'm sorry about Hollis. And your husband. How long ago did you lose them?"

"A number of years. Way before you were born. But don't be sorry for me. For a time, I knew two good people. Now they're gone. But there will be happier days ahead to heal patients, set bones, sew bleeding gashes. Tend to animals as well as humans."

"You the only doctor in Chickalookee?"

"Wish I were. We have two *gentlemen* who *claim* to be doctors. Some people swear by them . . . those who live. One shouldn't cut a tail off a dead cat. Other fellow's a fall-down drunk who wouldn't know a hangnail from a hemorrhoid."

"A hem what?"

"It's a bulge of swollen anal tissue. Up a butt."

I flinched. "How does somebody grow one?"

"Easy. You'll eventual develop a hemorrhoid if you strain when you poop."

I gulped. Doc had a blunt manner of speaking a thing out into the open. There didn't seem to be a false face on her. If it needed saying, Doc hauled it into daylight, hung it on a tightrope, and beat it like a rug.

"Been a long day," Doc said, bracing herself on the sink's edge, as though cramped. "I've treated a parade of disorders since breakfast—busted foot bone, swollen tonsils, colic, chicken pox, scarlet fever, food poison puke, back spasm, and a cinder in a welder's eye. Delivered a foal out a twisted mare. Then, before I could wash up, yanked Mrs. Mergott's fourth kid into the world."

"You looked whipped."

"Am. Let's go occupy those rocking chairs on my front porch and listen to the whippoorwills."

Outside, she kicked off her shoes.

I heel-and-toed-off my wore out boots, noticing that one stocking was offering my big toe some ventilation.

With her graying head leaning on the chair's high headrest, Doc closed her eyes. "Will you stay with me, Tullis? I have a room for you, soft bed, and clean sheets. But first, scrub yourself a bath. I don't tolerate dirty." Turning her head, Doc opened her eyes to look at me. "Can you stay?"

I nodded. "Got nowheres to go, ma'am. Nobody to go *to*. Here's like a dream. Can't believe you're willing to take in a cripple."

"Stop. No self-pity. You're young, able, plenty here for you to do. Learn to handle with eight fingers what most people are too clumsy to do with ten."

"I'll try, Doc. Honest will."

"Good. Tullis, you're well off, escaping a rodeo show and Judah. You are far better off than those poor, unfortunate horses."

"But they'll git a home. A meadow, Mr. Judah told us, to sort of retire in. He mentioned some sort of a kiddie camp."

Doc stopped rocking. "Judah fed you *that* story?"

"Ain't it true?"

"Nary a word of it. This morning, Wes Winchester stopped by to say farewell. He's on his way home to Redworm, where he and his sister still own their family ranch. Wes told me all. Threadgill is a Swamp County feedlotter who'll fatten the stock, including horses, for maybe a month. Then they'll be trucked to a slaughtery, hit in the head by a sledgehammer, and minced into pet meal."

Later, after a bath, I crept into the softest and whitest bed this side of clouds. Then lay awake the entire night.

# CHAPTER 11

W*HAM.*

 When the gun exploded in his office, Odessa Bob Swackert thought he'd got shot. With the deafening report still ringing in his ear, he turned to his addled assistant.

"Futrell . . ."

In a low, controlled voice, Sheriff Swackert spouted a spurt of unrepeatables.

Futrell Hoad Swackert, the dullest and dimmest deputy south of the Dixon line, sat staring at a smoking service revolver, as if pondering why his weapon discharged. All he did was squeeze a trigger.

Sheepishly, he looked at Odessa. "Are ya angry, Papadaddy? I'm sorry. I just sort of forget there was a round in the chamber."

With a moan, the sheriff opened the front door to flush the office free of the acrid odor of burnt gunpowder. What O. B. wanted to be flushing was his stepson. How in the name of sanity had he allowed Ulivia to persuade him to deputize her oddity of a offspring?

Futrell wasn't a bad boy. Nor was he the sharpest quill on a porcupine's posterior.

"Papadaddy, please don't take my gun away from me again and then make me check the parking meters along Exchange Street. The people notice my empty holster and poke fun."

"Futrell, it ain't exactly your empty *holster* that is wearing away my frayed nervous system."

"But the report didn't do no harm."

Sheriff Swackert panned his eyes around the office. Nothing on the ceiling except flies. He checked the walls. Ah! A bullet hole. There it rested, a little black .38 dot, plain as day, embedded into his latest wall poster, one that he had particularly pinned there for his deputy's edification. Its bold headline read . . .

# GUN SAFETY

"Futrell, hand me your revolver . . . *No!* For good-grief sake, not thataway. Don't point the dang thing at me. Tell you what. Just set it on the desk, right careful, without tickling the trigger."

"Do I git it back?"

"When and if you final develop the common smarts of a screwworm, maybe I'll again permit it to occupy your holster. Unloaded."

"What good'll that do?"

The sheriff smiled gently. "It may save lives. Mainly mine." Like trying to teach a toddler not to touch a hot cookstove. Odessa Bob sighed. Futrell for a deputy was burden enough. The humiliation deepened, however, when the Chickalookee citizenry referred to Futrell as "your son."

Slumping into his wool-padded chair, the sheriff applied his right thumb to depress the release lever, opening the six-shot Colt Police Positive .38 Special. Five unfired 158-grain cartridges fell out. Plunging the thin ejector rod expelled the single brass. He tossed it to his deputy, who dropped it.

"Here. Please allow me to suggest that you carry it in your pocket. Every day. As a reminder."

"I got a ex-cuse, Papadaddy."

"Never call me that again. Call me Sheriff or O. B. Years ago, your mother thought Papadaddy sounded cute. When you were a foot tall. At last measure, Futrell, you were six and a half foot, and still growing."

"Want to listen my ex-cuse?"

"Shoot. On second thought, Futrell Hoad Swackert, we have *shot* enough for one morning. Okay, lay your excuse on me." The sheriff held up both hands. "But don't skip over here and sit on my lap."

"But I'm sadly."

"How come?"

"I'm in trouble with Clemsa Lou."

Sucking in a gasp of panic, the sheriff asked, "Did I hear correct? You gotten Miss Clemsa Louise Wetmeadow in *trouble*?"

Futrell blushed. "No. Mercy, not *that*. What I mean is, she dumped me. Mama said I was to marry her up, but Clemsa's turning me down." Futrell's confused face posed a question. "She can't do thataway to somebody who was the high school cocaptain of a *football* team."

"What makes you doubt it?"

"Well, she said I was cute in my uniform."

"You look adorable." O. B. rolled his eyes. "And her casual compliment, in your mind, constitutes a eternal commitment?"

"Huh?"

"Miss Clemsa led you on?"

Futrell nodded. "Like a light switch. On, then off, then on, then . . ."

"No wedding?"

"Don't guess so, unless Mama can convince Mrs. Wetmeadow else. Another worry: Clemsa Louise said if her parents turn persisty, she might run away. To look for a daisy."

Smart girl, O. B. was deciding. Hope she doesn't skip town. Yet who'd blame her, with Ulivia and Emolly Sue calling the signals.

"To change the subject, Futrell, couple days ago did you telephone Doctor Platt, like I requested you, to inform her as to who's presently in custody here, as a temporary guest of Mosquito County?"

"I forgot. Sorry. You won't believe it, Papadaddy, but lately I just ain't been able to think too straight."

O. B. believed it. Picking up the black receiver from its horizontal telephone hook, he waited for a familiar nasal: "Number please."

"Hazel, it's me," Odessa told the operator, Hazel Glantz. "Be a darlin' and patch me into Doc Platt. Can't

58

remember her number. Thanks." He waited six rings. "Doc? Howdy, it's Sheriff Swackert with a neighborly call to inform you that we have a Mr. Hitchborn detained. Nothing deep. The Judge gave him thirty days for running a poker game on a Sunday. I hear His Honor was at the same table and dropped money. So please accept the department's apology for not calling sooner. Okay?"

There was a pause. A rather long one during which O. B. patiently waited for Doc's reply and drummed his fingers on his knee. Then he heard a sad voice.

"Thank you, Sheriff."

# CHAPTER 12

I couldn't eat my breakfast.

Doc understood. "Years ago," she told me in her quiet way, "whenever I was annoyed at my dear Frank, I'd clean. My mop became a sword and dirt was a dragon. Still works. If I'm blue, I bury myself in busy." Handing me a list of chores, Doc added, "Try it, Tullis."

"Yes'm. Anything you want."

"Got a personal errand," she announced, grabbing her pocketbook. "Make a dent in our duties, and we'll reward ourselves with a succulent supper." Doc winked. "Leftovers."

Although tired and still stormy, I waded in: scrubbed a frypan, applied steel wool to a shed hinge, then oil. Split stove wood. Filled the wood box. Burned trash and emptied ashes. Swept. Weeded a front flower bed and watered Doc's new Confederate jasmine vine. At the tail end of her do-it list was a tiny PS.

*If your hand cramps, quit.*
**A.M.P.**

Having free time, I decided to yield to temptation. Doc hadn't returned, so I visited my horse pals. As I arrived at the Stampede corral, the T. C. Threadgill flatbed truck was pulling out. Loose bales of hay had been dumped into the mangers and onto the ground. Threadgill was fattening the animals for slaughter.

Gripping the corral's top rail, I clenched my eyes tight shut, trying to dam up sorrow until I could blink it away.

With the exception of Signature, the stately white Arabian that Mr. Judah rode, but only before a crowd, none of these animals had names. Just brands. Nearest me, a red roan had been burned J33. But I'd always called this gelding Straw.

Slipping between the second and third crossbars, I joined my buddies, pleased how they left uneaten hay to greet me. Our final time together? Soon I'd come here to find a empty pen. A silent circle of ghosts. I recited the names I had given them:

**Straw**, a strawberry roan
**Clyde**, the gentle-giant Clydesdale
**Stocky**, a grullo, one white stocking
**Dapple**, a gray
**Sunday**, whiter than a hymn
**Bay**, a brown, with black mane and tail
**War Paint**, a pinto
**Signature**, a white Arabian
**Goldie**, a palomino blonde
**Ghost**, a spooky gray (no dapples)

**Albany,** a albino white, with pinky eyes
**Buck,** a burly buckskin, who really could
**Char,** a charcoal black mare

My unlucky thirteen. They deserved better than T. C. Threadgill's meat processing. How could I save them? Me, nothing but a broke eight-fingered kid. Like the horses, I was a nobody that someone had hung a name on.

'Twas a humid day. Moisture thick enough to scrape off a skillet and serve with a spatula. With my arms around Char's sweaty coat, I inhaled her strong female fragrance. All mare.

Had to be a way to rescue them. Think! My injured hand happened to rub Char's left shoulder, behind the muscle bulge, beneath her wither. Something. Not large, yet it was there in her hide. A rough scar.

Her brand. An old one.

While wondering why Char's mark loomed so uneven, the answer mule-kicked my brain. She'd been branded *twice*. Once legal, then possible stole, rebranded by a crook's hot iron. A shame to put a animal through that ordeal more'n once.

"Char," I whispered to her ebony ear, then lighter inside, "brace yourself, darlin'. A boy you know is cogitating how to steal you again."

Turning her head, the mare eyed me. "Do it, Tullis," I imagined I heard her nicker. "For every one of us. But not for money. That's plain wrong. Do it for *right*."

After stroking each of my loved ones a hurried so-long, I moved my boots back to Doc's place. She was there, tending a hideous rash on a crying baby, commanding the mother to quiet and help hold the child. The kid eventual stilled in Doc's cuddle.

"Hush up," Doc ordered the woman, "or else I'll charge you two dollars instead of one. I can't abide useless hysteria."

They left.

"That boring McCarty woman," Doc Platt barked. "Always telling how much she *worries*. Her child might prosper if she'd change it more often." She hauled in a calming breath. "I see you tackled your duties."

I nodded. "Doc, I got news. Not about you or me, but it has to do with our Stampede horses."

Washing her hands at the medical sink, Doc eyed my hands and tossed me the brown bar of Octagon. "Scrub." As I lathered, she warned, "They're hardly *our* horses, young man. Legally, they are the pathetic four-footed property of either Judge Hoad or T. C. Threadgill."

"Not for long. I just might steal'em."

For near a minute Doc didn't react, but then slowly shook her head in disapproval. "Let's meander to the kitchen. We'll be able to reason more clearly over a cup of tea."

Adding water to the kettle, I set it on a hot plate. "There's a place Wes mentioned, Doc, called Redworm. His sister's ranch is there. Half his." I thought it best not to tell her about the Redworm Rodeo, where I might earn a 8 buckle on a bull. "I'll drive my thirteen to Wes's place in Redworm, if I had a map."

Doc took white mugs from a cabinet, poured hot water on loose leafs of tea, added lemon. Then sat and sipped.

"That," she said, "is one puny plan. Chances are, being inexperienced in thievery, you'll fail. One person can't keep thirteen horses collected for so distant a trip. You will be spending much of your time gathering strays or getting lost. Perhaps get yourself shot by some rowdy who works for Mr. Threadgill's outfit, or the police."

"I'd git some of the other boys to pitch in. Trouble is, they all departed. We didn't even say a so long."

Doc balked again, insisting how tomfooly it was to commit a crime, ending me either in jail or dead. We argued, with Doc giving me reasons why my caper would crash and why I ought to give it up. Then Doc quit her sermonizing and, in a different tone, began to ask me questions, as though she were becoming interested. If not that, then fascinated, like a trapped rat eyes a snake.

Maybe it was my crazy imagination, but Doc seemed to be changing her tune. Then she started making suggestions on how stealing thirteen horses could be done.

"Well, you can't do it alone." Doc inhaled a long breath and let it escape at leisure. "Nor can I approve of your doing it."

"Maybe the two of us could."

"Stop. Stop. Let me think, Tullis." Raising her cup for another sip of tea, now cold, then lowered it. "I ought to be buckled into a straight jacket and have my brain examined."

I grinned. "Wow! You'll throw in with me?"

"Hold it. Didn't say I would, then again, didn't say I wouldn't. I'm in my fifties, and this is a big leap. A dumb idea."

We argued more. Doc suspected that with her or without her, I intended to steal the horses. Couldn't let'em die. Again she mentioned her age, a swollen ankle plus a assortment of aches. But I promised to ride the lead horse, and she'd follow in the rear with her Ford pickup.

"If we pull off this insane prank," she said, "we best make ready, early on. Plot a plan. An elderly woman and a brash young punk mustn't go gallivanting across South Florida in search of a bullet. Or a hang noose."

"Boy oh boy. We're taking a crack at it?"

Doc slowly nodded.

"Tullis, as of late my life's slipped into a rut. The only excitement in Chickalookee was the Big Bubb, and now *it's* folded. I haven't had a rip-snort adventure in two decades. So my answer's a probable *yes*. If we organize. Food, gear, a compass, bedrolls, and some detailed maps of the two counties. Redworm's in a north corner of Swamp County—a far piece. At least a hundred miles from here as a crow flies. You, me, and these horses aren't crows. We zigzag. So count on a hundred twenty."

Unable to set still, I was now jumping up and down, almost fixing to handspring a cartwheel.

"Whoa," she warned. "We need a third party. I refuse to go without one."

"Who?"

"Tullis . . . we require a professional *horse thief*."

I danced around the kitchen, almost spilling tea, until Doctor Platt pointed me to a chair. "How do we turn up a horse thief?" I asked her.

Doc rested her cup. "He's near. Within two spits and a holler."

"What's he like?"

"Charming. Endearing. A mix of magnetism and mayhem that could coax a smile out of Abe Lincoln's wife. But he is also a lazy, whiskey-drinking, card-cheating, skirt-chasing, nine-ball-shooting rascally reprobate. If anyone's carved a career out of thievery, especially horses, it is this sorry scamp."

"Where is he, Doc?"

"In jail."

"Do you actual know the feller's name?"

"Rubin Leviticus Hitchborn."

"How come you know this bum?"

Doc sighed. "He's my father."

# CHAPTER 13

E. Carvul Hoad belched an injudicious term.

"Woman!" he hooted into his telephone mouthpiece. "I don't give a red rat's rump how busy he is. Put him on! Even if he's busier than a one-arm juggler with poison ivy. Tell T. C. that Judge Hoad is on the line. Pronto."

His Honor didn't like waiting.

"Threadgill," he yelped. "You'd better soon answer your stupid contraption, or you'll be answering to *me*."

For near a week, The Judge had waited for T. C. Threadgill's check, one that he'd been told was in the mail, but had failed to appear. Who did this glue-factory horse hawker think he was dealing with, some flunky like Judah St. Jude?

"Z'at you, Judge?"

"Threadgill. Speak up!"

"Your Honor, I already sent the check."

"By mail or by snail? If the paid-in-full amount don't arrive at the Chickalookee Post Office by closing, you can expect my son-in-law, Sheriff Swackert, at your door by midnight to slap a subpoena writ on you so fast your nose'll bleed yellow."

"Nothing's come yet?" T. C. asked in a trickster's tone.

"Yes, something came to me. From you. And you dang clear know what. 'Twas a *feed* bill. Close to two hundred smackers for hay. Threadgill, you're charging me for fattening my own *dead meat*."

"Now let's not heat up, Elberton. If I'm not mistook, your stock is still alive on *your* Chickalookee property. So the bill's legal and binding."

"I won't pay it. Threadgill, you'll not wrench a red cent out of me. A deal's a deal. As I see it, they're already your critters. Not mine. And these show nags had better quit eating, or I'll march over to the Stampede grounds and smack a bullet into'em myself."

"Cool off. You'd be a idiot to whack horses that I won't take delivery on. Think about it. Financially, if'n you shoot yourself in the foot, folks'll be laughing at the name Hoad all over Mosquito County."

"When you coming for'em?"

"Soon's I locate a thirteen-hoss van. You're only a Justice of the Peace with no jurisdiction up here in Swamp County, so keep cool, Elberton. When I'm primed, you'll be duly notified. Not until. Hear?"

*Click.*

"That uppity sombee had the gall to hang up. On *me*, E. Carvul Hoad. Hah! I'll knock more'n a few spokes outta his wheels. Providing I can locate another buyer for mare meat."

The Judge kicked his wastebasket over, painfully barking a shin on the desk corner and producing a discoloring welt.

And colorful language.

# CHAPTER 14

—◆—

"How do I look, Doc?"

After I added another layer of reddy orange splotches to my chin, cheeks, and nose, she approved. "Like a rodeo clown. Luckily, this crazy costume of Chigger Dill's fits you to a *t*. You and Chig are twins."

For half an hour, Doctor A. M. Platt and I had been cruising Chickalookee in the cab of her Ford pickup truck waiting for Odessa to leave his office. Doc driving. Me scrunched down out of view. Doc told me about her father's useless life as a dishonest drifter. Also a gambler. However, when he managed to win one giant pot at poker, he banked most of his winnings into a trust fund, for her medical education. Doc figured she owed him a debt. Never knew how to repay him, because he was disappearing so often. Busting him out of jail would be her final attempt at trying to rescue him.

Biting a nail, Doc admitted, "That pa of mine has driven me crazy with worry. I'm more jittery than a two-tailed dog in a rocking chair factory. Can't believe we're to abet a jailbreak."

"You've got the easy part."

"True enough. Tullis, this is my first and final illegal act. If we pull our stunt and get away with it, we're going straight. We are retiring from outlawry."

The Ford must've hit a pothole, because it sudden bucked. My heart gasped, then subsided to its normal panicky pounding.

"We ain't criminals. We won't do dishonest to feather our pockets, Doc. It's a good deed."

"S'pose. But ol' Judge E. Carvul Hoad won't see it so kindly. That skinflint is the last person anyone in Chickalookee would dare to rob. Soon's he discovers what's missing, he'll even cable England to enlist Scotland Yard."

Doc's shoe switched from gas pedal to brake. Because I was bent into a ball and crouched down below the windows, that was my close-up view.

"Ah, there's Odessa, departing his office for a noon meal. Instructing his deputy." She slowed the pickup and parked. "He's driving away in the patrol car. Now's our chance to bamboozle Futrell." Yanking the *clickety-clickety* handbrake, Doc said it was time for me to come up for air. "Don't forget to limp, like Chigger do."

"Yes'm."

"Let *me* do the talking. Don't say *boo* until our good sheriff eventual questions you, and he certain will, about the chloroform. Then all you do is mumble. Or grunt. Pretend you're a dimwit. Odessa Bob's got a good heart. He'll give up and turn you loose. Until then, you don't utter a peep."

"I won't." In my pocket, I felt what Doc had supplied—a wee, corked bottle of sweet-smelling liquid, appearing to be water, wrapped in a soiled rag.

She crossed her fingers. "Our tomfoolery may not be brilliant, Tullis, but it's the only trick I can conjure to sneak Hitch out of the pokey. Course he'd be released in three weeks. However, our four-footed friends won't last that long."

Bolder than a brass band, but careful not to enter together, Doc and I paraded smack into the jailhouse office, disrupting a enormous, uniformed, open-mouthed deputy who was working a telephone. His flabbergasted face showed that he hadn't counted on a clown.

"Clemsa Lou, can I call ya back, Sugar? Why? Because the clown is here." Pause. "No, not a drop." Pause. "I *am* sober. Hang on."

Jumping up, Futrell dropped the phone. As he bent to retrieve it, and apologize to Sugar, I noticed that there was no revolver in his holster.

"Officer!" Doc trumpeted. "Where is Sheriff Swackert? I need to learn the whereabouts of a patient."

The deputy's face became instant alarm.

"We got a *emergency*?" he asked.

"Yes! I best go deliver a baby!" Doc made a curious face at me like we was strangers. "I'd presume your prisoner's expecting a visitor. I can't recall this rodeo clown's name." Doc leveled a warning finger at Futrell. "But *take no chances*. Lock'em both up. And hurry!"

"You're leaving?" Futrell asked Doc.

"Yes, so shake a leg, Deputy. A birthing can't wait.

72

I'll watch the office for you while you're down the hall."

"Uh . . . okay, I guess."

"If you hustle."

Confused, the large deputy obligingly lifted a ring of keys off a hook, opened a wooden door, and led me to the only occupied cell. Inserting the wrong key, he fustigated at the lock, changed keys three more tries, and swung open the barred door.

"Mr. Hitchborn, you got cumpnee." To me, he warned, "Mr. Clown Person, you're allowed ten minutes. I'll return to fetch you."

After locking us in the prisoner's compartment, Futrell returned to the plank door leading to the office. As he opened the door, I heard Doc Platt using a gushy voice.

"Deputy, you are *so* fortunate. Your sweet Miss Clemsa Louise Wetmeadow is *the* most *charming* young lady in Mosquito County. Cute as a bug. Now, young man, if I were you, I declare I'd get right back on that telephone this instant and . . ."

The door closed with a latchy *click*. Yet I'd overheard enough of Doc's oily pitch to make me almost laugh. So I faced my host. The iron clamp of aging had taken a purchase on him. At first I saw his face as a burnt-out hole in a tired blanket. An expression harder than a uphill haul.

"Mr. Hitchborn, sir?"

"Call me Hitch," he said, pleasant as a picnic. "Reckon you're in cahoots with Agnolia."

"Who?"

"Doctor Agnolia Moriah Platt, the daughter I forgot to raise." He held out a hand, and his smile baked me warmer than a smokehouse roof. "Thanks for coming." As I offered my left, we shook, and Hitch asked, "What's up?" Again he grinned as if enjoying the day. "I already like it."

"Quick," I whispered, "we have to exchange clothes."

"Deal me in."

"Soon as you're inside the costume," I said, pulling off my shirt, "I'll color your face with the gook that's smeared on mine. When the deputy comes back, keep mum. Once you're free, stay low, duck along the hedge around back, and follow the hardware store alley. Doc'll be waiting behind it in a blue Ford pickup."

He shot me a thumb-up. Hitch was savvy, even when I soaked the rag with chloroform and corked the bottle and gave it to him for keeping. Now in Hitch's clothes, as Doc had planned, I stretched out on the cot facedown, my head under the stained and naked pillow and my body beneath a blanket.

"Say," Hitch said, with a tap on my shoulder, "you forgot to clown up my face."

As seconds ticked by, I leaped up. Using my fingernails, I scraped the thick layer of goo from my face and transferred it to his. Not very neatly.

"You're a mess," I said, wiping my own hands and face clean.

"Always was, son. Whoever you be, thanks. Hope we meet again sometime, where there's women, rum, and music. I owe ya. One way or t'other, you'll be repaid."

Hitch didn't know how soon he'd settle the debt.

As the wooden door banged open and Futrell belted out a official "Time's up," I bounded to the cot, squeaking rusty springs, and again hid my entire self, keeping the chloroformed rag out of sight. But I could smell the stuff. The cell unlocked. From under the pillow, I saw Hitch raising a finger to his lips, begging silence, gesturing that I was asleep. "Shhhh," he hissed. As poor Futrell was escorting a clown out the door and into freedom, I grinned. A sly old fox, Hitch.

A few minutes later, I heard a wagon pull up and cut its engine. A distant door. Two male voices talking, then heating up. The wooden door cracked open a second before Sheriff Swackert thundered one dumbfounded word: "*Clown?*"

"Yessir, maybe that Stampede guy. Jigger or Trigger somebody. I seen him in the arena and he's a howl, popping out that barrel to haze a bull. He come here, and then he went."

Four boots scuffed along the cell row. So I placed the wet chloroform rag to my face, took a deep inhale, then another . . . had wild dreams until a hand grabbed my shirt—actual it was Hitch's shirt—and cuffed my face. But not hard.

"Hey! Wake up, kiddo." Slap. Slap. "You best come to. Hear?"

Opening an eye, I looked up at a very distressed and befuddled Sheriff Odessa Bob Swackert.

"Dang you, Futrell. Can't I go to the diner and

return to find a old-man prisoner still in his cell?" The lawman sniffed my rag. "You been drugged. Where's Hitch? How could he just saunter out of here? Who's this boy?"

"Beats me, Papadaddy. After you left, all I done was talk on the phone to Clemsa Lou. But she didn't believe me about the clown."

"Me neither."

Waking up, I was beginning to enjoy the entertaining conversation going on between the sheriff and his stepson. Had to grit teeth to keep from out-loud laughing.

"Futrell, you making up a story? Or are you serious saying that there was actual a clown in my jail? He walked in and then walked out, taking Hitch and leaving this feller?"

"Papadaddy, I swear. There *is* a clown around here."

Sheriff Swackert sighed. "Sure be."

# CHAPTER 15

"Well," said Ulivia, "I *hope* you're happy."

Odessa Bob Swackert winced. Another tirade. Whatever stupidity her son stepped in and then tracked into the house, Ulivia blamed her husband. One thing to be grateful for: their dining room table was long, removing Ulivia's dragon breath a merciful eight feet away.

"Futrell is such a *sensitive* boy." She added, "Now he's upset about Clemsa Louise, and if that's not heartbreak aplenty, then there's this clown."

"Please . . . please, Ulivia. Let's do supper in peace."

Ulivia threw up her hands. "Typical. Our only child is out there, in the patrol car, because *you* ordered him to search for a *clown*, one you admitted you never *saw*."

A forkful of his wife's delicious fried catfish was halfway to his hungry mouth. Then slowly sank. His stomach was begging for a Tums, yet he dared not leave the table.

"Rejecting my cookery?"

Hurriedly, O. B. lifted the fork again, chewed, and

smiled. "Mmmmm. It's super, dear." Truly it was, and he eagered to enjoy.

"Must you mumble with your mouth full?" She sipped water from a stemmed goblet. "Poor Futrell. Our lamb will probable be out there all night."

How, oh how much Odessa was wishing that he could depart and stay out all night. Better yet, for a week. Perhaps report home around the Christmas holidays, when Ulivia could become quite spirited. Even romantic. In silence, he gobbled dessert, wanting a second slab of banana cream pie, not risking to ask for it. So there he sat, fretting on how disgruntled his father-in-law would be. Hearing that Hitchborn had skipped, His Honor would hit the ceiling.

Or the fan.

During coffee, his wife said, "First thing tomorrow, best you contact Doctor Platt and find a few facts."

"Already called her. Only clown she ever treated was some ol' broken-down rodeo gink. But they all left town when the Stampede closed. Except for horses, the grounds are vacant."

"Well, my opinion," Ulivia snapped, "is . . . there is no clown. You're trying to cover up that a prisoner escaped *your jail*, a criminal who'd cheated my father at poker. Just wait until Daddy hears about this."

Holding his head in his hands, O. B. agreed. "I know, Ulivia. Believe me, I dread it like a dog in headlights."

"Not to change the subject, but our dear Futrell has been made a yo-yo for that . . . Wetmeadow hussy."

The sheriff folded his napkin. "Clemsa Lou's a charmin' young lady, Ulivia, and brighter than a brass button."

"You imply she's too intelligent for Futrell?"

"No. Just maybe Clemsa Louise is too smart to get married too young. Talk to her mother. Is not Emolly Sue one of your closest friends?"

"Hah! I originally *thought* such. But I can't rightly blame Emolly. Hard to believe we let Clemsa Louise get away. And a prisoner get away. Not to mention a clown, that nobody seems to know about." With a dainty gesture, Ulivia lightly patted her mouth with a napkin.

"There's still someone in the cell."

"You don't know who's in it?"

"A frightened mute in his middle to late teens. Can't talk. Drifter. A lanky boy with half a right hand who'd got chloroformed. No ID on him. Homeless, nameless, and crippled."

"Well, he's almost our son's age, I hear. Futrell told me that he thought this strange boy was feeble-minded."

Futrell would know, Odessa thought.

# CHAPTER 16

A cell cot ain't comfort. Yet it was good enough for me. Before joining the horse show, I'd bedded down in worse places.

Lying on my back with hands beneath my head, I digested the crispy chicken, potatoes, slaw, and peas that Futrell brung me on a paper plate from the diner. Plus chocolate milk! To pass the time, I recalled again and again how I was on top of Gutbuster, taking all the pain he could put on me. Stick. Stick. Stick for eight.

After convincing both the sheriff and his deputy son that I couldn't talk, no way could I inquire about release. Best I clam up and trust Lady Luck. Oddly enough, she come cantering to the rescue. The wooden door opened. Sheriff Swackert appeared, unlocked my cell—or rather Hitch's cell—and motioned me outward and into his front office. He sat down, and while he filled out a form, I glanced around, noticing a GUN SAFETY poster. I poked my finger into a little black hole.

It made Sheriff Swackert scowl.

He stood. "Son, whoever you be, you're at liberty.

Bird-free." He hesitated. "That hand a yourn ought to git looked at. If you don't bother, I'll drop you off somewhere in the patroller."

My insides bubbled with happiness as we rode. Not for long. I *almost* become history's first mute to scream out, "No! Don't stop here. Keep going!" because he'd braked at a familiar sign that read . . . Dr. A. M. Platt. Golly, if the sheriff knocked at her door, what would happen to Doc and Hitch?

But he didn't cut the motor.

He turned to me. "A good person, Doc is. Chickalookee couldn't survive without her. She'll tend to your hand." Pulling a dollar bill from his wallet, he said, "She gits a buck for office calls. Here you go. Good luck."

I leaped from the patrol car, then remembered that, like Chigger Dill, I ought to limp a little.

Closing the door, I itched to say a thanks. But I resisted and split him a grin. He offered a friendly two-finger salute on the brim of a handsome hat, eased his vehicle to gear, and rolled away.

Before I could reach the door, Doc busted out of it, threw open her arms, and hugged me. Then spoke. "Your face is filthy. Go wash."

In the kitchen Hitch sat at the table, occupied with two items—a mug of coffee and a map. He grinned. "Stand right where you are. I don't consort with convicts."

The three of us cracked laughter open like a morning egg.

"Hi, Hitch. I'm Tullis Yoder."

The old gentleman stood, rested a arm around my shoulders, smiled, and said, "Indeed you be. I recognize my clothes." Punching my arm—in a friendly way—he added, "Welcome back." He was a charming old coot.

Doc explained that she and her pa had matters to iron out and suggested I go see my loved ones. "Today," she said, "I visited a patient of mine, a produce farmer who owes me for medical services. In payment, I accepted a large burlap sack of carrots. On the back stoop. Present some to your pony cronies at the corral. I got a reason." Before I darted, Doc held me back. "Whoa. Best you shuck off Hitch's duds and get into what's on your bed, thanks to the Methodist Clothes Drive."

I thanked *her* instead.

"Another thing. Wear a hat, and wait until full dark before you sashay around in the open. Two people with badges might wonder why horses interest you."

"Yes'm."

"Report home in a hour. You're to log shut-eye, and no argument."

Impatiently I asked, "Anything else?"

"Yes, there is, Tullis. My distinguished sire is throwing in with us, and we're creeping out of town at three o'clock tomorrow morn. With thirteen companions."

Hitch threw me a wink.

A few minutes later, I pulled up, panting, at the corral on the deserted Stampede grounds. There they stood. My thirteen. Carrots make anyone popular among horses. Ducking through the corral rails, slowly, so as not to spook'em, I was eagerly surrounded by loving animals, making me feel warmer than a fresh muffin.

Clyde came to me first.

The Clydesdale had been Big Bubb's mount, and his black nostrils flared to recognize a familiar scent. A pal. To please Bubb, I'd given Clyde extra care.

More followed: Char, Goldie and Buck, Bay, War Paint the pinto. Then, as a side-by-side chariot trio of white: Signature, Albany, and Sunday; the grays: Stocky, Dapple, and Ghost; Straw, the red roan. All thirteen.

Each horse got a carrot.

The last carrot, Straw's, was extra long, and I bit off a short log to munch, so I'd feel like a horse. It snapped in my mouth with a crisp sound that defied the darkness. Although numerous clouds were masking the moon, I was able to detect a slight movement. A human form on the south side of the pen. Hunching low, I stayed behind horses, observing, worried that it might be the law. No. This shadow was too small to be Odessa or Futrell. I heard the mystery person moving closer and whispering to Sunday. I remained motionless. Now would be a poor time to be recognized. Or be friendly. There was no way I could say, "Howdo. I'm Tullis Yoder. Been in jail recent. Now I aim to steal these animals and skedaddle."

Still, I was cramping curious.

Peeking through Clyde's mane, I took a shock. Moonlight sifted down for a moment to reveal . . . a *girl*! So sweet a face. And easy gentle as she reached to stroke Sunday's nose. She wasn't made up glamour-gorgeous, not a Thalia June Soobernaw, more childlike. A doll who played with a hobby horse. Then the moon hid behind weather; the thickening night clouded me as well, because I was leaving Chickalookee. Never would I see her again, hold her hand, or learn her name.

How could I ever say as much as a hello to her? To brag to her that I was a rodeo bull rider.

It made me stop chewing the carrot.

# CHAPTER 17

E arly morning. Almost three o'clock.

Wearing her blackest funeral dress and bonnet, Doc Platt stepped aside to watch Hitch soundlessly unbar the corral gate. Tullis was inside, baiting the band with carrots.

Hitch's idea about wardrobe made a rhyme of reason; the three of them would dress only in black. No problem. Doc's husband, Frank, rest his soul, had been an active church deacon, pallbearer, usher, and a lay preacher. Luckily, Doc had kept a few of Frank's clothes. A storeroom closet had provided complete attire for both Tullis and Hitch. Even two dignified black hats.

Enticed by the carrots, the horses quietly followed their lead black mare and matriarch, Char, who also willingly carried Tullis on her bare back. In file, the thirteen sleepy animals calmly left the abandoned Stampede area, and strolled past the snoring burghers of Chickalookee. Due east. Only Tullis was mounted.

Following the band of horses, a hundred yards behind, Doc Platt drove her Ford pickup while Hitch sat beside her. Aided by a tiny flashlight and magnifying glass, Hitch squinted at a county map.

"He was on target," Hitch told her. "Our boy promised that the black was dominant over the other mares and geldings. By the way, a stallion never leads a wild band. Leastwise, not here in Florida. A stud'll usual drive from the rear, nip at stragglers, but the band follows what wranglers call a mother mare."

"So we're the rear guard. Where to, O mighty stallion?"

"A few miles. Up ahead, a poker pal of mine, Leroy, runs cattle. Soon's we bend north and arrive at his place, you go back home and sleep. Come back to the ranch late afternoon. If Leroy has what we're after, usual does, then Tullis and I have chores to take care of."

"And what are we after?" Doc asked, controlling the pickup in low gear, at about three miles per hour.

"Color change. A gray horse'll dye to brown if we rub its coat with crushed butternut husks. And, if you steep the gallnuts of ragweed, it produces a blue dye, to darken a white horse to gray. For variety, add a few patches of butternut and the result will be close to a skewbald."

Doc shot her father an amazed glance. "No doubt about it. You really are a professional horse thief."

"Thank you." Hitch smiled warmly. "It's grand to be good at something, dear daughter. I'm proud that you practice medicine. My special talent just happens to be distruth."

Lightening her foot on the accelerator, Doc slowed

the pickup to maintain their distance from the band.

"We can't go from ranch to ranch, can we?"

"No," said Hitch.

"Then how shall we hide?"

Before answering, her father folded the map. "Agnolia, tell me something. Why do you think that I suggested we all wear black?"

"To blend into the night."

"True," said Hitch, "but there's a second reason. My dear, sometimes the simplest way to hide is to be obvious. To holler, Look at me!"

"I don't follow."

"Well, there's one particular town we don't fix to avoid called Pittman, to use as a decoy. We pass through it. If we try to tiptoe into it at midnight, chances are we might git caught and collared." Hitch held up a finger. "But, if we parade through at noon, making noise, no one'll suspect we're crooks. Best part is, we reverse our route, to throw any pursuers off the scent."

"Interesting. What *will* they suspect?"

"In our black togs, and with a banner that says The Lost Tribe of Jehu, we beat a drum, sing hymns, and loudly pray for the spectators. They'll accept us as a religious sect. Perhaps pity us, because we are lost and searching for Jehu. Or the Almighty."

Doc groaned. "I give up. Who in the deuce is Jehu?"

"Hundreds of years before Christ, there lived a ancient king of Israel, who, according to any comprehensive dictionary, was a rather reckless chariot driver. And a horse nut."

Doc shook her head. "I don't buy it. Neither will anyone else."

Hitch's elbow gave her a knowing nudge. "It's a scam I've worked a dozen times, without fail. Agnolia, they'll not merely believe we're religious, they shall also be convinced we are truly lost, pity us, allow our horses to graze on their meadow grass, and serve us a supper."

"You actually intend the three of us to work this flimflam wherever we go, town after town, until we are caught and confined?"

"Nope," said Hitch. "If'n we do this dodge more'n once, chances are that it'll fail on the second go-round—a blunder that has bilked many a bunko artist. Trust me, daughter. Your father's a cultivated crook."

Doc sighed. "Please, one favor . . ."

"Name it."

"Resist," she said, "sharing too much of your unlawful lore with Tullis. I think he has a chance to turn out proper."

Hitch grinned. "You mean instead of a horse thief like you."

# CHAPTER 18

Wham! . . . Bang ! . . .

In uncontrolled rage, The Judge triggered his double-barrel shotgun, aiming at loose dirt in a vacant horse corral. Fumbling to reload, he was hell-bent on waking the entire town.

Although today was a court day, E. Carvul Hoad was a picture of anything but a jurist. He wore a stained nightshirt, a ratty gray bathrobe that even a moth would reject, and one slipper. Only minutes earlier, at dawn, the ever-reliable Ethel Smertz, who always took an early morning walk, had awakened him with an earsplitter of a phone call, reporting the Stampede horses as missing.

"Nothing such as this ought to reasonable happen," he whined. "How dare people sleep while I am being robbed?"

Glancing at his car, he glowered.

In his rush to reach the Stampede grounds, His Honor had raced his DeSoto too eagerly and had braked too slowly, crushing a fender on a gatepost. Now, hopping on his single slipper, The Judge tried to extract a sandspur from between his toes. His bathrobe's belt, hanging by only one loop and trailing on the ground, tripped him. He tumbled facedown into dried manure.

"Dang your rotten guts, Threadgill. This mess is your doing. I'll curse your hide into a tannery and throw you in prison for fraud, conversion, trespass, contract violation, theft, wanton destruction of property"—he felt his sore toe—"and personal injury."

T. C. Threadgill's check had never arrived. Plain to see that the slimy snake had pulled a fast one. Sneaked down here in the night and swiped thirteen head. Already back in Swamp County, slaughtering, destroying evidence.

Staggering, The Judge stood like a stork, trying to balance on one skinny, hairless shank of a leg, whiter than a dried antler. Unable to catch his balance, he danced on the needle-sharp sandspur that continued to prick like a Sunday conscience.

"Bread and water for you, Threadgill. A life sentence with no parole." He continued yelping threats into the uncaring atmosphere. Blinking dust from his eyes, The Judge hobbled around the entire pen, shotgun ready. "Where's our sheriff?" he wailed.

Dirty and exhausted, he trudged toward his spanking-new, baby blue DeSoto sedan, a paint choice he hadn't favored, but Ethel said matched his eyes. Miss Ethel was a clever woman. Perhaps too clever. However, at the moment, The Judge was tempted to fire his son-in-law, Odessa Bob Swackert, and pin a badge on Ethel Smertz. Only the town might gossip. Ulivia would stir up a storm.

"Instead of waking me, why hadn't Ethel telephoned Odessa Bob direct? Or did the sheriff already know?"

Approaching his vehicle, Judge Hoad was also approaching a conclusion: Odessa Bob and Ethel could be secretly in league with the Threadgill crowd. Ganging up against him. Well, now he was wise and wary. Trust nobody had always been his motto. "If your own mother comes to visit with cookies, check her ID and make *her* eat the first one."

The DeSoto refused to start, causing him to slump behind its steering wheel, more defeated than a parched weed.

Morning brightened. Chickalookee was up. People would be everywhere. How could he leave the automobile and walk home in a bathrobe carrying a shotgun? Folks would think he'd gone loony. Besides, a thug would recognize his empty car. Judges have enemies galore. A person he'd fined, or confined, might swing a crowbar at his new car and demolish it.

"Drat. I don't deserve this. Wait until I get my mitts on Threadgill."

In a flash of fury, the Justice of the Peace shattered the peace of everyone within earshot by honking his horn. One long-lasting blast that never quieted was bound to bring the sheriff. Of course he'd prefer Futrell.

"I'll tell him my horn got stuck."

# CHAPTER 19

After I slid off Char's black back, she continued to walk beside me, content, her soft muzzle near riding my shoulder.

Horses are night sleepers. But we'd robbed ours of several hours' rest. In about fifteen miles, according to Hitch, we'd meet up a L Lazy L outfit, owned and mismanaged by a lifelong crony, a Mr. Leroy Loller.

Morning began to chirp yellow. Ahead of us the easterly dawn lay across a wide horizon, a wavy serpent of light broken by stands of cabbage palms, each a tall naked trunk topped by a fuzzy ball of fan fronds. Plus black grackles and brown thrashers. A horse blew a snort, a mockingbird was showing off a variety of trills and whistles. A fresh Florida day, minted gold, frosted with a silvery dew.

I smiled.

What else could a orphan boy wish for? Except maybe a girlfriend, and the ability to grow two more right-handed fingers.

As Hitch predicted, we passed between a pair of gray

wood poles, connected overhead by a twiggy arch that informed of our whereabouts. In the arch was an odd sort of a triangle.

Took me a few blinks. It was Leroy Loller's brand: L Lazy L. We kept going for maybe a mile into fog, early mist blanketing a lush meadowland, a steamy quilt of wet wool. Looming ahead, a shack roof and sheds, square fences and round corrals.

A dog barked a warning.

Behind the grayish mongrel hound, a human shape appeared under a cowboy hat. A rifle—or maybe a scatter—was held in a elbow crook, ready yet not threatening. He was a large man. Burly shoulders, as solid built as a Methodist hymn. His weapon never changed its downward aim, although its owner advanced two steps. Then another.

"Good morning, sir. My name is Tullis Yoder," I said. "If you're Mr. Leroy Loller," I added, thumb over my shoulder, "back yonder's a friend of yourn, Mr. Hitchborn."

He cuffed back his hat.

"Hitch?" He paused in disbelief. "Sober this early?"

"Yessir."

"Well I'll be gelded."

We shook hands. Mr. Loller's fingers seemed to grip hardness, a plenty of outdoor work. Around each fingernail curved a brown ring of ranching.

"Sir, is there a enclosure I can please lead my animals into? Or maybe a fenced-in graze?"

Mr. Loller didn't balk. "Why not." He gestured to his left. "Swing open the white gate. Once the band's entered, close it. Tight. Stay inside to gentle'em until they settle. Plenty water in them troughs, so let'em fill. On strange turf, a thirsty horse'll spook sudden, and I don't cotton to repair wire or wood."

I followed his orders.

With wisdom, Doc didn't bring the Ford forward until the horses were contained. From inside the pen, where I was rubbing War Paint, I saw Hitch jump out and trade easy punches with Leroy. Doc waved a tired arm, circled the pickup to drive toward Chickalookee. Probable to complete a night's rest. But she'd return.

We went inside the shack, a one-man junkyard. Soiled plates and undersoaped laundry. No sign of a Mrs. Loller. Over the black cookstove, a sagging string drooped a pair of socks that needed drying and darning.

Leroy burnt us a real belly buster of a breakfast. Prior to eggs, fatback, and jellied toast, I was the only male who bothered to soap. Leroy prepared cookery by wiping one hand on his stained shirt while the other hand wiped his nose. Yet there were no complaints from me. The eats arrived hot and plentiful. The coffee must have got drained out of a truck engine's crankcase, hefty enough to float a anvil, kill weeds, or poison rats.

"Want more grub?" Hitch asked me. "Youngster, if you was a leaf, you'd barely be more'n a stem and veins.

How about some extra eggs?"

I yielded to the offer of more hen fruit, and in a minute or less, Leroy dumped another greasy pair on my yellow-smeared plate. "Here ya go, Tullis. Dirty on both sides."

While the old-timers dusted off old times, I heated a pan of water to attack pots, pans, and eggy plates. Cigarette smoke thickened. The conversationing between Hitch and Leroy was entertaining and educational.

"You recall Virna Bidwell, the one we called Bedroll?"

"A smile as wide as her hips. Claimed her teeth was real, but I learn that Virna's gums had more china than a half of Hong Kong."

"Bedroll had a kid sister. Her name was . . ."

"Hortense. I never forgit a gal with dimples, and she let me count hers. Forty-nine, and a plenty in pervoking places."

"Whatever become of Hortense?"

"Well, she retired. Sent away for a mail-order course to study and become a postmistress. Hortense split my ear with a table leg when I told her she was ideal for the job . . . except for the *post* part."

In a sentimental mood, Hitch rubbed a tore earlobe.

"You actual counted forty-nine?"

"Would I fib?"

"Say, I disrecall, what was the year you'n me drove cattle for that Pan Handle outfit?"

"It was 1903. Or half a hour later."

"That greedy town marshal took after us for sporting his bowlegged wife. So we said if he'd forgive the charges, we'd allow him to ride herd all night. And keep every calf that dropped."

"Yeah, and by next morning, not even one calf got born, because the entire herd was all steers."

"The last laugh was on you. But I can't remember why you got tossed into the Gnawbone jail. What did you do?"

"Well," said Hitch, "seems like I fell into financial disfavor, due to my investing funds on fast women and slow horses. The lady judge was a former schoolmarm, and she insisted that my report card flunked me a F . . . in penmanship class."

Leroy raised a eyebrow. "Penmanship?"

"Yup. My pen wrote a bad check."

# CHAPTER 20

"Sheriff office."

Odessa Bob Swackert eyed his stepson. At least there was one minor duty that Futrell can perform. Unassisted, he could answer the telephone. Almost correctly.

"Yes, ma'am. This here's Deputy Swackert."

Sort of half listening, the sheriff perceived a female voice with a lot to say, but it was too early in the morning to wonder who was calling at this hour. O. B. hadn't yet tasted his mug of coffee.

"Yes'm . . ."

Resting a polished size-twelve snakeskin boot on his desk, O. B. leaned back on his swivel chair; he heard the springs squeak. He'd have Futrell apply oil. No, on second thought, his stepson might ignore the spring and lubricate the seat cushion. Or his own knee.

"He is *where*?" Futrell asked the caller.

Odessa shrugged. Loose dog, a kitten up a tree, or a cow strayed off-meadow partaking peas in some spinster's garden.

"It won't start," Futrell said. "Sounds to me like she's

gas-flooded. Or it could be the carb.”

Mildly amused, O. B. was doubting that the deputy would know a carburetor from a carbuncle, even if he found one under his pillow. Futrell would probable suspect the Tooth Fairy.

“Nightshirt and bathrobe. Okay, I’ll . . .”

Setting down his coffee mug, the sheriff controlled himself enough to inhale, deeply, because something weird was hatching. None of what he was hearing made a lick of logic.

“Shotgun,” said Futrell.

Staring up at the bullet hole in his GUN SAFETY wall poster, O. B. vowed not to panic. Yet some precious odd ingredients were bubbling in this pot. Unable to make out precise words, he heard the woman’s hysteria rising to emergency pitch.

“He refused to ride in your car,” Futrell recited with a nod. “Yes’m, I do understand, Miss Ethel. Meant to say Miss Smertz.”

A gagging mouthful of hot coffee spurted from Sheriff Odessa Bob Swackert’s nostrils, splattering his pale green necktie and two unlucky lapels.

“Yes’m, he’s right here to the office.” Pause. “No, I won’t tell him, Miss Ethel.” Longer pause. “A tow truck? Will do. And I’ll personal come to the Stampede grounds. But first, like The Judge said, I’ll git Papadaddy to arrest . . . you know.”

O. B. was on his feet.

“Futrell, best you lend me the telephone.”

“Okay, here ya go. But she done already hung up.”

Hearing the faint buzz of a disconnection, the sheriff calmly replaced the receiver on its hook. "Judge Hoad wants me to arrest . . . *who*?"

"The feller what stole the Stampede horses."

O. B.'s heart almost stopped. "Stole the horses? They're *gone*?" He paused to suck in a desperate breath. "Did she, or The Judge, mention a particular *name*?"

Futrell smiled. "Threadgill."

# CHAPTER 21

"Emmett," said Doc, "these are ideal. There definitely is a bristle or two of divine artistry in your paint brushes."

The print shop smelled pungently of ink, lacquer, varnish, and kerosene-soaked rags, and there were assorted stacks of cardboard plus rolls of canvas. On the walls, examples of typefaces and design garnish.

"Thanks, Doctor Platt. Appreciation of our professionalism is always welcome, especially from an honest person like you."

Honest? She had the urge to shrink into a floor crack and hide from shame.

Standing across the Quick-Sign counter from its proud proprietor, Doc nervously inspected the identical pair of ten-foot banners that Emmett Foster had painted to Hitch's specification.

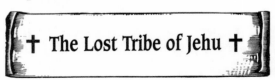

✝ The Lost Tribe of Jehu ✝

"No charge, Doc. It's on the house. I support any Holy Word movement whenever possible. By the way, Doctor Platt, when did you mention this'n here Jehu Revival was coming to town? Gertrude and I might like to attend."

"Soon as we know the exact date, Em, you and Gertrude May will be the first folks I notify. And bless you for your generous contribution to the Faith."

"I usual claim that a soul-cleansing experience don't always last. But my Gert says neither do a bath, but once in a spell we all need one."

"Gertrude's right about that," Doc agreed, still burdened with guilt. Then, tangling even deeper into Satan's web, she asked, "Em, whatever happened to your American Legion marching band?"

"A shame." Emmett Foster fingered a vanished clarinet. "We broke up. Gibson Clark, who was our lead cornetist, lost his lip. In a poker game. Get it? Ain't that a howl?"

"A hoot. Y'all still have your instruments?"

"I don't. Gave the ol' licorice stick away. But, as I recall, Calvin's got a few. Cal Boothmire." Em smirked. "Fixing to take up the tuba are ya, Doc?"

"No, but I know of some youngsters over in Tarkoosi that are forming a band. What they need is a pair of cymbals, a slide trombone, and a big bass drum."

Em slapped the counter. "You're in luck. Cal's my brother-in-law. Hang on. I'll ring him on the contraption, and say you're on your way over, and to dig 'em out and dust 'em off. Corner of Elm and Pine. They might's well toot *somebody* a tune."

"Thank you, Emmett. The church is obliged."

"Forget it. Say, how come you happen to be wearing a black dress? It ain't Sunday. Or has my calendar converted to Chinese?"

Pretending a pained look, Doc said, "I must attend a funeral. Not here. It's up to Swamp County."

"Oh. Somebody die?"

Brilliant question, Doc was thinking, yet she succeeded in remaining solemn. "My father. Dad passed away in his sleep. For years, he was an acquaintance of our good Sheriff Swackert's. I can assure you that Odessa will be shocked to hear the news. As will Judge Hoad."

"Sorry to learn about it. A pity." Emmett shook his head. "What did your dear father expire of?"

"Horse fever. Not to be confused with *hay* fever."

Emmett's eyebrows lifted. "Horse fever? Well, you're a medical person, and study up about such." He scratched his head. "Me, I never heard of it."

"Until recently, neither had I."

# CHAPTER 22

F ollowing the breakfast cleanup, I searched Leroy's
tack room and located a burlap sack of dried corn-
cob, stiffed to prickly, and used about a dozen to curry
the mounts. Their undercoats had turned thatchy with
thick mats of coarse fur that brushed out free in fluffy
wads.

"That'll feel you better," I told Goldie, our palomino,
who enjoyed a scratch more'n a hog shouldering a sty
post.

Nearby, Hitch and Leroy had teamed up, mashing
the husks of butternuts to produce a bucket of brown
gunk. They also steeped a batch of ragweed nuts into a
blue dye.

"We got enough," Hitch said.

Standing there reveling in the refinements of horse
theft, I figured that coloring the horse flesh would be
a three-man occupation. Wrong. Their plan appointed
*me* to supply the elbow grease. The burden of bossing
was saddled on Leroy and Hitch. At first it wasn't too
labory. Leroy fished out a banjo, tightened a string or

two, and plinky-planked it, while Hitch tortured a pocket harmonica.

It turned out that the coonhound was quite a judge of music; he set to howling until Leroy kicked him.

Meanwhile, I plastered Dapple and Ghost, both grays, with butternut goo. They didn't become bays, as I couldn't blacken their manes or tails, yet they surely did brown like fresh-baked bread. Being so busy, I never noticed that Leroy fetched a jug. Wasn't sarsaparilla. But drinking it enabled both men to endure their own sorry music. Their singing could've convinced a dead rat to run away.

*Oh . . . the . . .*
*Higher up a bramble bush,*
*The redder grows the berry.*
*The more you kiss'n spoon a gal . . .*
*The more she'll tease to marry.*

Over and over, they tormented the song; sang it and played it. Hitch actual played it on the harmonica by blowing through his *nose*.

"Why do it thataway?" Leroy asked.

Hitch winked. "Any feller who noses a harmonica will never worry about anyone else asking to borrow it."

The little sleep I'd enjoyed had gutted my gumption, but I ordered myself to whack it through to the end: "Tullis Yoder, best you finish your job, because neither of these ol' coots could stand up long enough to take a leak."

Mustering all the bowel I had, with a dab of ragweed blue on Sunday, Signature, and the pinky-eyed albino, Albany, I managed to turn three white horses to gray. Earlier, I'd shucked off my black shirt so's not to sweat it sour. Upon finishing dye duty, my chest, neck, and arms seemed to belong to someone from Mars. Or a coal mine. Above my belt, I looked to be one big bruise.

Washing didn't help. Horse dye goes *on* but it doesn't come *off*. Leastwise, not easily. Made me wonder if'n it soaked in permanent.

That was when Doctor Platt showed up in her Ford, hauling food, oats, more clothing, and another sack of carrots. Plus some strange objects under a canvas. In a blink, Doc studied Hitch, Leroy, and their jug, which now lay on its side without a cork. Seeing my five repaved animals plus my new skin color, Doc spoke not a word. She strode to the shack and returned, carrying a broom.

In their booze-befuddled stupor, Hitch and Leroy greeted her with thick-tongued mirth. Nudging one another, they tried to entertain her with one of their corny old vaudeville routines.

Leroy: "Hey, where ya been all afternoon?"

Hitch: "I went fishing with Boopsie."

Leroy: "Catch anything?"

Hitch: "Good golly, I hope not."

Both men busted out in guffaws. I didn't get the joke; and, from the look on Doc's face, she wasn't loaded for laughter. Advancing to where Leroy and her father rested in the shade, leaning against a shed's wall, with barely a fleck of dye on either, Doc cocked her broom and, full force, let them have it. She whacked a blistering to both my bosses. Any one of the blows might have knocked out the champeen boxer, Mr. Joseph Louis Barrow.

Finally, when Leroy and Hitch hurt too much to holler, she cracked the broom across her knee and threw the pieces at them.

Wearing a sly grin, I figured that Doc's tantrum was targeted only at the pair of geezers. A moment later, however, she came storming my way, hotter than a busy pistol. Boiling, eyes aflame, Doc grabbed me in a gizzard-popper grip and hauled me to a flat board outside the shack. Leroy's excuse for a washstand. Using a mixture of lye soap, sand, and grit determination, Doc attacked every inch of my discolored skin, removing the stubborn butternut, ragweed, years of grime, several layers of my hide, and possible a few vital organs. I got sudsed, scrubbed, rubbed raw, and rinsed, twisted, and then hung out to dry.

To pay Doctor Platt for her trouble, I made a big mistake by telling her, "A bull rider don't have to be this clean."

The wrong thing to say.

For the remainder of that day, Doc Platt's icy mood would make the North Pole shiver. Not one to bend, her rigid spine stood stiffer than a hickory doorjamb. Soon as a moon added cream to a bittersweet chocolate sky, Doc, Hitch, and I thanked our host for hospitality, collected our thirteen four-footers, and took leave.

Leroy Loller didn't beg us to stay, in spite of Doc's presenting him a dollar so he could buy hisself a new broom.

Moving into darkness, none of the three of us were speaking to the other two. Doctor Platt, her sobering father, and me, the scrubbed patient, seemed to face in different directions.

Three claws on a turkey foot.

# CHAPTER 23

I n night shade, Hitch moved among the horses.

They had stopped and were now thirty miles away from Chickalookee, Hitch reckoned. Maybe more. Hours ago, he insisted that Tullis take his place, riding the pickup with Doc Agnolia. The boy had balked, professing he wasn't pooped-out spent, but Hitch knew otherwise. Day or night, the young crippled hand rarely rested but tended and groomed and cared for thirteen friends.

Standing beside the War Paint pinto, hands on the animal's back, Hitch rested his head, inhaling the welcoming warmth. A strong and steady smell. Now, nearly dawn. Eyes closing, he wondered if he'd been asleep on his feet with Paint for a pillow. Was the animal also sleeping?

Speaking of pillows, Hitch figured that he might possible sneak to the pickup and sort through his duffel bag. For a pillow he could use that clown costume, the one in which he'd escaped from the Chickalookee jail. Earlier, he had wondered why he'd bothered to pack it. Well, perhaps one more disguise might come handy.

An owl hooted its hunger.

Repositioning his shoulder, a sharp twinge of deserved dolor made Hitch wince, then smile. Agnolia Moriah Platt could belt a broom. Squinting at the Ford, he could barely make out Tullis and his daughter, both asleep.

A short distance from the hobbled horses, Hitch folded himself down to a inviting spread of pine needles, on his side. Funny, he mused, how a horse'll sleep standing and will lie if it's a foal or, like himself, old and about through.

He slept until his daughter shook him.

"Good day, Agnolia. What time is it?"

"Ten. If you intend to detour us around Pittman, we missed out on a covering darksome." Through with her nagging, she walked away.

Rising to his feet, Hitch felt as though every muscle was aching, plus bones and joints. Even his hair hurt. Luckily, he had only a few strands. Tullis came over to say howdy.

"Here's my ploy," he explained. "Instead of avoiding Pittman, we strut straight through it, knee-deep, and save a few souls. Mainly ours. We're short of food, so instead of sponging off Leroy—"

"We sponge off Pittman people."

Hitch nodded. "Time is come, Tullis, for you and me and Agnolia to employ our banners, loosen up the musical tools, the ones my daughter so thoughtfully provided, and toot Pittman a tune."

——◆——

# CHAPTER 24

"What a relief," said Odessa Bob Swackert.
How refreshing to sit behind the wheel of a
Mosquito County patrol car and abandon Chickalookee
for a day. Here he was, crossing the county line to invade
a neighboring territory. As he motored into the first
town in Swamp County, a tastefully designed sign read:

```
┌─────────────────────────────────┐
│ ┌─────────────────────────────┐ │
│ │                             │ │
│ │       WELCOME               │ │
│ │     TO FORT DEE             │ │
│ │                             │ │
│ └─────────────────────────────┘ │
└─────────────────────────────────┘
```

His father-in-law, Judge Hoad, hadn't an ounce of
authority here. Not a gram of clout. Fort Dee was T. C.
Threadgill's turf. Red warning flags were waving in
O. B.'s mind. As a Mosquito County law enforcement
officer, he really had no official business poking into another sheriff's jurisdiction, which also included Gnatfly,
Pittman, Dead Goose, and as far north as Redworm.

Best he contain himself and tactfully soft-pedal his
every maneuver.

A courtesy call to the Swamp County Municipal Building would be a must, with a friendly howdy-do to the badge in charge. Sheriff Theron Flowers had wisely wedded and bedded Threadgill's niece. In rural Florida, if you hustle somebody, you risk provoking such person's entire clan. Kin, cousins, and unchained dogs.

No need to rush.

First he'd have himself a look around.

O. B. slowly drove to the T. C. Threadgill Stockyards. Animals aplenty, plus a smell to match, and a constant lowing of thousand-pound steers impatiently awaiting being shipped to slaughter. He noticed three groups of penned horses, none of which matched the detailed description that Ethel Smertz had aptly provided. So he stopped to idle his engine and to question a dirt-covered yardy.

"How long these animals here?"

"Couple three weeks."

"Got any recent arrivals?"

"Nope. I been working here at Threadgill most my life. So I'd know if'n fresh meat unload." The man took note of O. B.'s police vehicle.

"Thank you, mister. Oh, by the way, you happen to see a little elderly man, late seventies, name of Hitchborn?"

The yardy shook his head.

"How about a clown?"

"Beg pardon?"

"Well, a sort of rodeo clown. Some claim he walks with a slight limp." O. B. felt fooly by asking. "By

111

chance, maybe he was with a skinny boy, under twenty, with half his right hand missing."

"No dice. None of them peoples."

"Thanks, anyhow." O. B. touched the brim of his Stetson. "Sorry to be a bother."

At least Odessa had absorbed a bit of information. Action had to be taken. Part of his job. O. B. could still hear The Judge's snarling command of early this morning: "Go git'em."

Returning into the center of Fort Dee, he parked in a visitor space at the municipal building. An impressive structure. Two stories. Grunting up a dozen concrete stairs, he entered through a revolving door to seek his Swamp County counterpart. It was irksome that Sheriff Theron Flowers had such a posh office, larger, far spiffier than his own cramped jailhouse corner in Chickalookee.

To boot, Flowers was a good ten years younger, and possible fifteen. There's no justice in law enforcement.

There sat a secretary to screen visitors. Another thorn. And, to hammer the jealousy spike deeper, she was a perky blonde. Cute as a cub.

"Sir," she warbled, "may we assist you?"

Removing his cowboy hat, O. B. said, "Ma'am, I am Sheriff Odessa Bob Swackert from down south in Mosquito County. Would the good Sheriff Flowers happen to be in?"

She buzzed. O. B. waited, yet not with extreme patience. After a minute, an apple-cheeked Theron Flowers appeared with a smile and a handshake. "O. B., glad you found Swamp County." It was a poke at his lack of geographical savvy, which Odessa ignored. "I hear you enjoyed a scenic tour of the yards." His smile widened. "News travels faster than a patrol wagon."

"I was sort of hoping to enlist the advice of Mr. Threadgill, but there wasn't a car outside the stockyard office."

"T. C.'s got more hustle than a honeybee. Even busier now, trying to collect thirteen Stampede animals. A van drove to Chickalookee but rattled home empty."

Odessa said nothing. But he didn't buy the story. How clever of T. C. Threadgill to dispatch a van to fetch a band of horses that he possible knew wouldn't be there. Slicker than sly.

Theron said, "There's another tasty tidbit. We heard some aging inmate escaped the comforts of your jail-house. What's going on in Mosquito? You boys sponsoring a crime wave?"

O. B. tried to laugh it off. No sense in grilling Sheriff Flowers beyond manners, because he'd learned what little he'd come to uncover—the horses weren't at the. stockyards. With a polite nod to Miss Delicious, and a cool handshake to her smart-alecky boss, O. B. departed.

Theron walked him to his vehicle, overly gracious, but not without a parting jab. "Lucky you won't have to campaign a reelection."

With a sigh, O. B. headed for home, suspecting Mr. T. C. Threadgill quite a measure less.

And suspecting Hitch a lot more.

# CHAPTER 25

M otoring into the Chickalookee terminal, a Penin-
sula Omnibus Company cruiser rolled to a
smooth stop.

The diesel belched exhaust as if it needed a rest.
While the brakes hissed, the door folded open, squeaking, parting its black rubbery lips. Five passengers exited.
After supervising her green flowered suitcase being
stowed in the baggage bin, Clemsa Louise Wetmeadow
happily boarded the bus for a fifty-mile pleasure trip.

Her mother waved.

Then, cupping hands to her mouth, her mother
shouted, "Now please remember, Clemsa Lou, to telephone us the minute you get to Harriet's." This marked
her fifth time to say it.

No window seats were available. An elderly woman
in a hideous veiled hat festooned with red berries, wearing a pansy frock, looked the girl over carefully and
reluctantly moved a gigantic pink purse to free an aisle
seat. Clemsa Louise had barely sat and settled when her
bad-breathed seatmate, in a piercingly high and abrasive

voice, introduced herself.

"My dear child, I am Miss Nettie Thurl. And if you want my advice, you're rather youthful to be traveling alone. It doesn't look proper. What's your name?"

Unable to resist, Clemsa said, "Ginger Millerton. But at the pool parlor where I rack balls, my gentlemen customers, for short, call me Gin Mill."

"My word." Nettie forced a swallow. "You going far?"

"Just to Nome, Alaska. It's a day trip."

Since high school graduation, Clemsa had been clerking in Woolworth's, a five-and-dime store. Having earned a few days off, she was about to visit her favorite fun-loving relative, Aunt Harriet.

Clemsa thought it best not to reveal to her mother the real reason for the trip, that being to elude Futrell Hoad Swackert, who kept hanging around, uninvited, whining more sorrowfully than a lame hound. And, too often, bringing that bossy mother of his, Ulivia. At the bus station, Clemsa Louise Wetmeadow had made a considered decision. When the ticket booth lady had asked, "One way, miss, or round-trip?" Clemsa heard herself say, "One way, please."

Aunt Harriet would understand.

Clemsa watched the varied palmettos of Florida blur by. Roadside shrubbery was frequently blanketed by the many mounds of leafy greenery, temple upon round-spired temple of kudzu. What a place to hide! Yet she truly felt liberated. Fresh faces. Freedom.

"How long," Nettie Thurl persisted to investigate,

"will you be away from Chickalookee?"

"A short stay."

"Your family, are they church people? Not that it's any of my business, but I don't do any truck with apostates. These days, nonbelievers are lurking everywhere. The shameful impiety of these transgressors. Hellions. Doing the Devil's deeds. Tempting, tempting . . ."

Glancing over her shoulder, Clemsa was *tempted* to change seats. Or perhaps pull back the sliding glass window and push Nettie out. However, a more entertaining idea crept into mind.

Torment was a double-bitted axe.

"Miss Nettie, I told you a story. Because I drink whiskey and take dope, not to mention my hootchy-kootchy dancing at the pool parlor, I am *forced* to leave town." Clemsa's hands clutched her abdomen. "You know the usual excuse . . . to *visit my aunt*. Aunt Elmer. Named after her mother."

"My stars."

"But it's doubtful I'll reach my secret destination, to meet my sweetheart lover who's an escaped criminal. A bank robber. He won't never get to make me an honest woman."

"Why . . . why not?" Nettie Thurl asked in a wavering voice, now holding her purse with both hands.

Clemsa leaned closer and whispered, "Look behind us. Three or four seats back. Those two men are *white slavers* who are after me for cheating them in a crap game." She whispered, "And selling them naked pictures of our minister's dog."

Nettie peeked, then hurriedly faced forward, trembling. "Yes, you're right. They sort of do look foreign."

"Mongolian mobsters. In cahoots with Al Capone. Now when I escape off this bus, please promise me, Miss Twirl, that you won't sneak back yonder and strike up a conversation." Again she whispered. "Aunt Elmer says people like that carry knives."

"Oh . . . oh, my Lordy be."

"A pity they've seen you with me. And worse, being seen could ruin my chances of getting accepted into Yale Divinity School." Clemsa had another wicked thought. "If you're opposed to divinity there's always penuche. Or fudge."

The amusing game that Clemsa Louise was playing with Miss Nettie Thurl made the time, and the scenery, fly by. Sooner than expected, the bus stopped at another depot.

Their driver loudly announced the town.

"Pittman!"

# CHAPTER 26

Oh, the prank we played on Pittman.
Though we were generally headed north with the horses, Hitch insisted we enter Pittman *not* from the south end of town. So we circled to approach the town from the north end. The first leg of his Pittman plan.

"When we leave town," Hitch said, "we do the reverse. We exit heading south, half circle again, then continue north, toward Redworm."

"Ah," I said, "everyone in Pittman will agree that the Lost Tribe of Jehu was traveling due south. If the law comes looking for us, Pittman people will all be pointing south as we move north."

"You got it," Hitch said with a slinky wink. "It's a decoy move."

Our pious processional into Pittman was headed by Doctor Platt, in a black dress and bonnet, driving her Ford at the speed of a lame snail. Our two freshly painted banners had been prominently posted on both flanks, enabling the slow reading, open-mouthed onlookers to ogle . . .

# ✝ The Lost Tribe of Jehu ✝

Comfortably trailing the pickup, gently guiding thirteen horses of seldom-seen shades, Hitch and I, in black, solemnly courted everyone on both sides of the street, speaking only, "Bless you, Brother," or "Bless you, Sister."

Approaching the open sandy area that tried to be a village square, Doc braked to a stop. Hitch and I soft-hobbled horses that already had been watered, oated, and carroted to quiet. Then, with our instruments, we tortured the ears of the town's music lovers with a well-known gospel hymn, "Rescued from the Burning Flames."

Wisely, we had rehearsed a number of times, so that Doc's trombone, Hitch's cymbals, and my giant drum would mix passable. To my ear, our blend didn't sound the least bit melodic but more like a foundry or a factory. As we played, another miracle. Scores of ungifted voices actual sang the words with Hitch and me.

*Oh . . . how . . .*
*Poker chips and scarlet lips were*
*Darkening my life.*
*Cigarettes, and race track bets I'd owe.*
*Then I sight a shining light to*
*Guide me from the strife.*
*Rescued from the burning flames below.*

*Fetch, fetch, fetch . . . this*
*Poor pathetic wretch, from*
*Sin and gin and all gin rummy games.*
*Vice isn't nice . . . it's*
*Worse than shooting dice.*
*Save me from the Devil's burning flames.*

*Oh . . . how . . .*
*Billiard balls and dancing halls were*
*Blackening my soul. I was*
*Even reading Edgar Allan Poe.*
*From despair, a golden stair would*
*Snatch me from Hell's Hole.*
*Rescued from the burning flames below.*

Had this ancient anthem's composer heard our instruments and choir, I doubt his departed soul would have rested in peace. It'd pick Purgatory over Pittman.

If the singing was sorry, the sermon was sorrier. The Reverend Hitchborn mounted the roof of Doc's pickup, cleared his throat, then slowly raised his hands to beg silence. Citizens calmed. The only noise I could hear was the roaring rumble in my stomach. Bull butterflies in battle.

Pittman's popping eyes now focused on the Reverend Rubin Leviticus Hitchborn as he raised his black-sleeved arms to the heavens.

"Hear ye! Hear, O troubled transgressors. Listen to the Word and be thereby cleansed into righteousness by the Book of Jehu. Hearken, all ye of feeble faith. . . ."

On and on and on Hitch pulpitized.

Head bowed, I secretly stole a sideways peek at Doc's concerned face. Faith in her father's foolery was stretching like a second-hand girdle. About to snap. Her eyes closed in prayer. But I'd wager she wasn't praying to Jehu or to any other fakery that Hitch could manufacture out of malarkey. Doc knew her pa like a foot understands a fungus.

The people of Pittman stood statue still. In awe. Unprepared for such a spate of scripture, especially outdoors in the center of town.

"Hear ye, good people of Pittman. Whoever doth graze the swift steeds of our prophet, Jehu, and house or supp his poor charioteers, who stand now before ye, shall be forgiven, sanctified, and bestowed a hallowed home. We are pilgrims. Lost. The only home we hope for is *yours*. So throw open thy gates. Donate oats or hay to Jehu horses. Share with us the broth of your table. And for absolute purification . . . bring us both bread and *wine*."

"Hold on!"

Turning, I saw a preacher-type of gentleman approach Hitch, level a finger, and confront the shepherd of our flock.

"I happen to be a ordained minister who knows the Holy Bible inside and out. There's no such Book of Jehu."

Doc crossed her fingers. Earlier, she'd told me that she knew no one in Pittman, nor would they recognize her. Yet she was adjusting her black bonnet to hide more of her face. As for me, I just stood there, feeling my backbone yellow, fearful that I had gotten my good doctor friend into bad trouble.

"You're absolutely right, Reverend," said Hitch. "It is the only Old Testament book that got washed overboard off Noah's ark. That, kind sir, is why we are the Lost Tribe. Yet we search not for the book itself, but for its benefactorial *guidance*."

"Amen," someone assented.

Hitch took his turn to point. "Your good minister is *correct*! You won't find any Book of Jehu in the Bible. But you certain will locate Jehu in your public library's master dictionary, the one that weighs twenty pounds."

"Is that true?" Someone wanted to know.

"If, I say *if* Jehu is not there," Hitch said, pointing at a dark and threatening sky, "confiscate our holy horses. Tar'n feather me. Hang me from your tallest oak. Throw my body in a snake swamp. In fact, *burn my truck!*"

I heard Doc gasp.

Their minister nodded. "Amen. This upright pilgrim tells us the truth. I can always spot a honest face."

A crack of thunder convinced the crowd.

I winked at Doc. She looked at me, wordless. Didn't have to speak, because all of Pittman was sudden repeating "Amen," and scattering like leaves in a breeze.

But not before a few souls herded our horses to pasture, and brung us into their hearts and homes. Each of us went to a different house. I was luckiest; at my place, there was only two other people, and one was a right pretty gal. About my age, but a inch shorter.

The other person was her Aunt Harriet.

# CHAPTER 27

"Flu," said Doc.

"Sister Agnolia, you a doctor?"

With her hand pressing a cooling cloth to the little Nugent boy's brow, Doc replied. "A few of the faithful say so. What I am is a *healer*. There's no charge for benevolence, and I refuse to take even one Pittman penny. I'm grateful that our Lost Tribe saves youngsters from the jaws of pneumonia, using natural remedies. Mustard, goose grease, and sumac root. For a hacking cough, hang a bag of camphor around his neck."

Mrs. Nugent quickly telephoned her sister. The Word traveled fast. Especially *no fee*.

Before Doc could thank Mrs. Nugent for the overnight bed and wave a farewell, several neighbors appeared, bearing ailments and requesting her powers. Cheerfully, she obliged, as this was her true calling. A chance to ply her profession and think of herself as a dedicated doctor of medicine.

Not a horse thief.

For a wheezing child, catnip tea. A dose of castor to

eyes and ears for easing the bowel. For headaches, a chew of willow bark, horseradish, or beet greens. Heart murmur? Garlic. Rub mullen leaves on a pale face. Croup? A tincture of vinegar and beeswax; and if croup sudden attacks at night, steam a child with the vapors of Florida pine turpentine and whiskey.

"Don't panic," Doc advised a lady who seemed overly distressed at a new freckle. "My dear, learn the difference between toast burning and the whole house on fire."

"Your two brethren, the preacher and the young one with a sorry hand, are they also gifted with magical powers like yourself, Sister Agnolia?"

"Not exactly. We are of varied talents. Our reverend is a savior of souls and mental distress. Tullis, our disciple, is a charioteer like Jehu."

Prior to leaving Chickalookee, Doc had consulted her own dictionary, and in the *J* section, tripped over *Jehu*. As Hitch had insisted, there he was! An ancient king of Israel and a charioteering enthusiast of speedy steeds. Hitch's command of the English language was more practical than impressive, yet the basic savvy was there within him. Hitch read books. Perhaps he'd share biblical knowledge with Tullis. Teachings from the top. Instead of dealing from the bottom.

What troubled Doc deepest was the nagging notion that Tullis might abandon her advice to join some ruinous rodeo circuit. No doubt, this lad was naturally tempted by the urge for identity, to become a *somebody* rather than an unknown nobody. Beyond proving his boyhood among boys, Tullis was aiming to establish his manhood among men. Rodeo men. Rowdies.

Tullis Yoder's belt hungered for an 8 buckle. And to obtain one, he'd willingly risk becoming another Kicker Zell.

# CHAPTER 28

I tried not to burp. Or worse.

Holding back wasn't easy, because of the bountiful breakfast I shared with the pretty young lady, Miss Clemsa Louise Wetmeadow, and her jovial Aunt Harriet. Expressing thanks, excusing myself, I started to head for the horse pasture, but was surprised and delighted when Clemsa Lou tagged along.

Like usual, the horses greeted me ears up, so eagerly that I momentary forgot Miss Clemsa. Turning, I observed her arms were folded as though harboring a suspicion.

"Brother Tullis, my tootsy." With a knowing smile, she added, "The three of you bible wallopers are the Lost Tribe of Jehu about as much as Aunt Harriet is training to pitch for the Brooklyn Dodgers."

I stopped stroking Signature.

"Furthermore," she said, "if that fast-talking old coot is an ordained clergyman, I am Bobo the Dog-Faced Ape." Her voice lowered. "Yesterday, as y'all came whizbanging into Pittman, I knew where I'd seen these horses. In Chickalookee, whenever problems cornered me, I'd visit them at the corral."

The girl was truthful.

"Yes, I seen you there. A few nights ago." I sighed. "Please don't blow a whistle on us, Miss Clemsa, or at least wait until Doc and her daddy take leave of Pittman. Then I'll take full blame. But my two partners ain't young no more. The shame of jail might do Doc in."

Praying she'd string along, I looked up at a sunny morn sky that was blossoming into puffs of buttery-edged popcorn. I recalled being a little hungry kid who'd longed to taste a cloud.

Clemsa laughed. "Brother Tullis—is that truly your name?"

"Don't guess I honest know. Got no parents. But I answer to Tullis Yoder." I smiled. "Rhymes with odor."

"Only if you let it."

As she lightly rested a gentle hand on a mare's wither, I hankered to touch the same horse but didn't, fearing it wouldn't look proper. Without any talk, we sort of floated among the band as though it was a garden, offering affection to each animal, breathing a bouquet of four-footed flowers.

"We stole 'em away." I explained. "It was either that or they git slaughtered for pet food. So I roped Doc into my thievery. And, in turn, we busted Hitch out of the Chickalookee jail."

"My," she said, "you've been a busy boy. When y'all leave Pittman, what's next?"

"Another fifty miles north, to Redworm."

Her face brightened. "The rodeo!" As I nodded, Clemsa announced, "Aunt Harriet and I are going. We're staying at the General Redworm Hotel. By the way, she's known and respected Doctor Platt for many more years than have I and recognized her yesterday. I'd guess those two old friends might plan a Redworm reunion."

"Gee," I said, "that'll be nifty."

"Don't worry," Clemsa told me. "We won't squeal."

"On behalf of the horses," I said, "thanks." Not knowing what else to say, I offered my left hand, and we shook, like friends. Eyeing my right, she asked me about it.

"Bull."

"Searching for suicide?"

"No, just itching to stick on a bull for eight seconds. Then I'll quit for keeps." Displaying my crippled claw, I added, "Don't reckon I'll ever play a piano."

"Another goal you're itching for?"

"Yes'm. I'd love to make my own music."

Stooping, she selected an object from the ground, straightened, then showed me a tiny brown segment of a fallen pinecone. "Know what this is, Tullis?"

"A pine wing."

"Right. But also a seed. A fresh beginning. True, you won't be playing a piano. But pinch this in your right hand, like a banjo pick. Your left hand forms all the chords. I bet with enough practice you could teach a banjo to cook supper."

As she handed me the pine wing as a keepsake,

Clemsa's eyes sparkled like new dimes. But I was hoping she wasn't smelling my sour shirt or all my years of barnyarding. It might be polite to back up a step and apologize.

"Sorry I'm so soily."

"Although I have known you less than a full day, Tullis Yoder, you seem wholesome of heart and cleaner than the first bite of a wedding cake. Perhaps my aunt and I will see you in Redworm. Good luck."

When she walked away, I was worrying that this could be the one and only time I'd ever be close to Clemsa Louise Wetmeadow. Well, no sense in mooning selfish wishes that couldn't possible come true. Right now, my plate was piled with problems.

Two senior people and thirteen stolen pets. They were all at the top of my thinking and ahead of any other matter.

Including belt buckles.

# CHAPTER 29

VILPERT.

It was the final name at the tail end of Sheriff Swackert's to-call list. A pencil line had been drawn through all of the other people, as they hadn't helped a iota. Nor had yesterday's trip to Fort Dee.

"Hazel, sorry, dear lady," he apologized to the telephone operator, "but I need one more try. Please ring my cousin, Vilpert Rodham. He's up north in . . . golly, I forgot the place."

"Looty Creek?"

"That's it. Bulls-eye!"

O. B. drummed impatient fingers on his desktop and waited for Hazel Glantz—who amazingly knew of most everybody, including their dogs, cats, and canaries, everywhere in Florida—to plug in a connection. A voice that was shaggy with sleep rasped a hoarse "Hello."

"Vil? Hope I didn't wake you and Miss Contessa."

"No matter. Ain't been resting too good lately. Indigestion. Maybe I ought to cut back on acidy chow. Unless I dose myself with pepsin at bedtime, I'm up half a the night trying to pass gas, and it bothers the woman awake as well. Night before last she throwed the clock at me. Shelby Wittermann had a like trouble, until he made Shirley wear a wristwatch."

"Doing any bass fishing?"

"Not regular. But some the fellers been hooking keepers outta Lake Mildred. Fourteen-, fifteen-pound big mouth. Hittin' on plugs. Y'ought to come up'n visit and wet a line." Vilpert paused. "By the way, who'm I talking to?"

"It's me, Vil. Your second cousin."

"Clarence?"

O. B. sighed. Why were all the Rodhams so simpleminded? "No, on account Clarence died more'n ten year ago. This is Odessa down in Chickalookee."

"Who?"

O. B. tried not to yell. "Sheriff Odessa Bob Swackert here in Mosquito County. This'n is kind of a *official* call, ya might say, to glean some information about a suspicious person, name of Hitchborn. Cardsharp. Carries a photograph of Miss Faye Blackstone in one shirt pocket and, in the other, a harmonica."

"Clarence played the harmonica, didn't he?"

"No, that was Gooch Fillpot, who lived behind him. As I recall, Clarence sawed a fiddle and rattled spoons. In fact, he used to—Vil, before you hang up, we are missing some valuable horses here. Got stole."

"About how many?"

"Thirteen."

Vilpert laughed. "Funny you should mention that.

131

Because just yesterday, I had to crank up the Studebaker and carry Contessa to her beauty parlor appointment."

O. B. was confused. "Is this about horses?"

"Well, I'm coming to that, so keep your pants on. Contessa don't favor the way Gladice Murdock blues her hair. Gladice owns the hairdresser saloon here in Looty. So, once a month, I drive Tessa out of town, and that's where we happened to almost run over all them Jay-Hoo horses. Right on the main street. I'd estimate thirteen. We didn't stop to count because Contessa don't cotton to reporting late at the beauty shop."

"Where? Where were you?"

"You know, the same place where Contessa always goes to frilly up and gets her hair blued, even though it cost fifty cents extra."

"Vilpert, this is important. Which town?"

"Where else? Pittman."

# CHAPTER 30

The Lost Tribe lit out of Pittman like it was on fire. We didn't go quietly. Quite the contrary. Again, I credited Hitch with a full scoop of sneakery. For two reasons: First, our exit was so earsplit, rattle-bang loud that we attracted scores of citizens to watch and wave a farewell; second, we made our escape *due south*, asking how far it was to Gnatfly, the opposite direction of our Redworm target.

"But twixt here and Redworm," Hitch told me, refolding Doc's map, "you'n I might do a detour into a entertainment area that's less'n a mile distant of Dead Goose."

"Why?" I asked.

"Emergency," Hitch whispered. "Got me a lady friend in Tickletown who runs a rowdy house." Hitch's smile stretched wider than the mouth on a jack-o'-lantern. "She wears a firetruck red ruffle dress. On her face there's more colors than a pinball machine and looks like she'd cuddle in a cactus patch."

"What's her name?"

"Fauna . . . and her establishment is called The Night Crawler."

"I never visited one of them . . . places," I confessed to Hitch. "And not certain that I'd gumption to go."

"High time ya did." Hitch elbowed me, then lowered his voice to a hiss. "Tonight, when Agnolia's asleep, we'll whangdoodle over there, shoot us a rack of nine ball, irrigate our innards, and hoot up a holler with Fauna and her fillies."

"How'd she earn a name like Fauna?"

"Well, years ago, when she first claimed to be Flora, I told her that she looked a lot more animal than vegetable. So I renamed her Fauna."

Hitch continued to tout the assorted glories of Tickletown, a genuine Florida tourist trap, designed by its inhabitants to soak every sucker that passes through.

For the remainder of the day, it was impossible for me to look Doc straight in the eye. The black vulture of vice perched on my shoulder. To skedaddle off with Hitch might lose me what little decency I'd earned.

South of Pittman, we bent a half circle and moved north. Every step I was dreading Tickletown, and if Miss Fauna had greeted me face-to-face, I'd have run up the tallest timber.

To match my morbid mood, the afternoon brought a sour sky and blowsy weather. Tree leaves turned belly-up. When it rained, I wanted it to rinse me of tarty thoughts. Guilt buried its horny head into my flesh like a chigger bug. Alone, beneath the storm, I hid among my horse friends, while the two older people sought shelter in the Ford's cab.

Hitch and Doc entertained themselves by harmonizing, their voices blending almost as pleasing as two cats yowling on a back fence: "Life's too short to polka with a ugly man."

The rain abated, leaving a wet odor, clammy as a cold supper. You could carve the air with a knife blade and taste mildew. But gradual, Florida dried my face with her warm towel. Foliage was rejoicing, celebrating sunlight, and each leaf was a shimmering emerald. Once again, the yellowy sun cooked on the sky's great griddle like a single fried egg. We continued north another mile and pulled to a whoa in a stand of tall pines. A fragrant spot. Even the smell was cool.

Feeling clean and pure, I made myself a promise. If old Hitch suggested that we sneak off to that Tickletown place to yahoo mischief, well, I wouldn't play no part in it. Mr. Hitchborn would have to go lonesome. To visit a place such as The Night Crawler would seem sorry.

Besides, I wanted to earn Hitch's admiration as well as Doc's trust. To stand firm on this might be a step in that direction. No way I could force Hitch to honor me.

But at least I'd respect myself.

# CHAPTER 31

Nobody recognized him or knew his name.

Until recent, he'd been a celebrity back in Chickalookee. Crowds had cheered his entrance into the Big Bubb Stampede arena, wearing a spangled costume and mounted on Signature.

Unfortunately, those highfalutin glory days had abruptly ended, chopped by the merciless machete of mortality.

Big Bubb's death.

Judah St. Jude squatted atop a cheap blanket that he'd spread on the board sidewalk of the main touristy thoroughfare of Dead Goose. In place of a cowboy hat he wore a rag turban in which he stuck a dozen turkey feathers. His face and hands dyed brown with butternut juice. Rather than rhinestones, he wore a fake Miccosukee Seminole outfit festooned with strings of colored beads.

He called himself Chief Panther Bear.

Surrounding him on the blanket lay a peace pipe, a turtle shell, a cow skull, bat-wing soap, a gator-claw back scratcher, cactus tea, lucky sand, a possum passion potion, love petals from a moonvine, bumblebee wax, holy mustard seed, clam salve, rat yeast, pox-free tobacco, holly herb, armadillo hair-restorer, moth liquid, bluebird egg tonic, larva lotion, and stinkweed. Plus a long cow horn, with a hidden kazoo inside, that a tourist could blow through to honk a disgusting noise and that he described as a Seminole Indian war trumpet.

Yankee tourists, vacationing in Florida, would buy *anything*, including petrified goat sweat. And worse, take it home in their suitcases, wrapped inside a shirt that stated . . .

## I been to Dead Goose.
## And you ain't missed nothin'.

An hour ago, Judah actual convinced a city slicker that a dried, hollowed-out bull scrotum was a genuine Seminole water canteen. Five bucks for an object that smelled like a crotch. Recalling this particular sale made Judah St. Jude inflate with pride. Very few people had his natural talent to con. Most men couldn't sell a broad on a battleship.

Pushing the fiver into his pocket, Judah drew a deep breath. But delayed an exhale. His nostrils detected a very memorable sensation. Not unpleasant.

Looking left and right, Judah saw only automobiles plus assorted delivery trucks and vans. Except for a sleeping cat, not a single animal in sight. Yet he couldn't be mistaken, not after spending decades around rodeos and horse shows. Filling his lungs a second time, he paused. Yes. There it was.

Horses!

A whole band of them?

Bending quickly, he grabbed the four corners of his display blanket, collecting his array of junky merchandise into a bulging, clanking sack. "A hunch," Judah told himself as he dogtrotted, beads rattling, down a side street. A slight breeze met his face, wafting the animal aroma. Definite. Becoming stronger as he ran.

Turning a corner, he saw . . . Signature.

His Arabian gelding was no longer white but a strange blue-gray. He counted thirteen head. About right. He easily identified the pinto, then others. Parked nearby, an unoccupied Ford pickup. Walking nearer, he could make out Mosquito County on the license plate.

"Chickalookee, to be exact," he said quietly, observing the first three letters on the tag—CHK.

Disguised as Chief Panther Bear, he ran no risk of being remembered, so he dared several paces closer to assess this succulent situation. One by each, he recognized the Big Bubb Stampede stock. Several had been clumsily recolored, so it was obvious that a slippery deal was in progress. Judah salivated for a piece of the profit pie.

About to leave, Judah stopped for a final squint at the band. A youth in a black shirt was moving near a charcoal mare, talking to her, brushing her mane with what appeared to be a crippled hand. Hadn't there been a boy in the Stampede crew who'd been so injured by a bull?

Yes. Judah recalled assigning a scrawny helper to tend to Bubb.

Couldn't be the same boy.

The horses, Judah was suddenly thinking, ought to be with Threadgill in Fort Dee. But they were here in Dead Goose. Somebody had turned a trick, and the smell of money was now stronger than manure.

A minute later, short of breath from rushing, Judah St. Jude arrived on foot at a local Gulf gas station, then politely inquired if he might borrow the telephone. He was coolly met by a mechanic in greasy trousers and a shirt that stated his name: GUS. Looking this beaded and befeathered absurdity up and down with a wary eye, GUS shook his head.

"The boss," he said, "don't usual entertain strangers, and not no Seminole savage who's winded from running away from something. Maybe the po-lice."

But when Judah stuffed a dollar bill into GUS's pocket, GUS weakened, yet warned him to keep the chitchat brief.

Giving the operator a Chickalookee number, Judah waited, and then was rewarded with the familiar voice of Ethel Smertz. "Judge Hoad's office."

"Ethel. It's me. How ya doing?"

After a pause of stony silence, Ethel's reply turned even colder. "I presume you'd prefer to talk to The Judge. At present, he's occupied with a visitor. May I tell him the purpose of your call?"

Judah choked back a hanker to spit. Or tell her off. Was this uppity woman the same gal he used to order

139

around and send fetching? However, best he clamp a lid on lewd language. Ethel Smertz might prove usable.

"Thank you. Perhaps you can advise me, Ethel, so's we won't have to disturb His Honor. Do you know, my dear, if he sold the show horses, and if so, who to?"

Pause. "One moment. The Judge might wish to confer with you personally." This consideration preceded a longer pause, and then . . .

"Judah?" The raspy voice of Elberton Carvul Hoad crackled in his ear. "How gentlemanly decent of you to take the time in your busy schedule to keep in touch with a dear ol' friend."

Friend? Judah, inhaling gasoline fumes, was wishing that GUS would quit staring at him and go crawl under a leaky transmission.

"A quick question, Your Honor. How would you like to learn the immediate whereabouts of a certain band of thirteen animals that, until recent, was in corral in Chickalookee?"

Following an unsavory expression, Hoad said, "I don't guess you're fixing to tender this information *free*, to a elderly public servant. For old times' sake."

"Not a chance," Judah was sore tempted to reply, but refrained. Aloud, he said, "If Your Honor approves, I'll meet Sheriff Swackert, up here, in a hotsy-totsy called The Night Crawler. It's close by to Dead Goose in a place called Tickletown. Got that? Ten o'clock tonight. Oh, and please supply Odessa Bob with a sealed envelope containing my reward. In cash. Let's call it a finder's fee."

"Fee?" Hoad snarled. "Gimme a number."

"Well," Judah sweetened his voice, "seeing as the pair of us used to be beer buddies . . . fifty bucks. So, if that's acceptable, ten o'clock tonight at The Night Crawler. I shall willingly offer the information soon as Odessa forks over the—I mean, extends Your Honor's gratefulness."

"Okay. Fifty smackers. Not a nickel more."

Judah St. Jude was smirking. "Fifty . . . per horse."

# CHAPTER 32

In his musty and paper-cluttered Fort Dee office, T. C. Threadgill was not in the merriest of moods.

Earlier, he had received word from a Redworm business acquaintance, Mr. Ashbel Colpippin, that the upcoming Redworm Rodeo was seriously short of stock, namely show horses, for the parade.

"Well now, I got a plenty of pretty ponies," T. C. had lied to Ash. "How soon you be needing'em?"

"Right away sudden."

"Good. Please allow me to get back to you, Ashbel, because you're in luck. We just maybe got a dozen. So sit tight."

Trouble was, T. C. didn't have any to trade. Nary a one. Sheriff Theron Flowers, who had married T. C.'s niece, had already reported the thirteen Big Bubb nags as missing. Stolen. Now T. C. had hisself a buyer, but no cussed horses. With a wayward spit of Red Man, he missed the cuspidor a foot short but didn't give a snort.

"Dang it! Colpippin's desperate. If'n I could grab a holt of all them Stampede critters, on price, I could press poor Colpippin against the wall."

His eyes slowly narrowing to slits, T. C. began to wonder: Was it possible that Judge Hoad was pulling a antic and maybe stole his own horses, in order to sweeten the pie? Or maybe collect some insurance?

"Wouldn't put it past him. E. Carvul Hoad is crooked enough to hide behind a bent corkscrew."

On his desk, the black upright telephone was ringing, but T. C. allowed it to continue bothersome, presuming it was Colpippin calling back in a sweaty-palm fret, and no doubt expecting delivery. He took his time lifting the receiver from its horizontal fork.

"How do."

"Is this Mr. T. C. Threadgill?"

"Who wants him?"

"Someone who could wangle a profitable exchange of thirteen horses, show quality. I know where they be. The people that's got'em ain't the bonafide owners."

"Where they at?" T. C. asked, not expecting an answer.

That oily voice! T. C. was recalling where he'd heard it: At the phony fat-cowboy tourist trap down in Mosquito County. The gink calling was Judah St. Jude.

"Their exact location, Mr. Threadgill, is what I'm dealing. But we better move sudden. Meet me in the Silver Spoon Diner. It's in Dead Goose, quite near Tickletown. Let's say around nine o'clock this evening. And I presume you'll bring cash."

Why not? T. C. already had a business appointment in Pittman, and Dead Goose weren't more than two

143

hoots and a holler away. However, T. C. had heard that Dead Goose, after dark, turned into a whoop-de-do town. Full of grifters. If carrying cash, it'd be prudent to take along some muscle.

For example, Sheriff Theron Flowers.

"Nine o'clock," T. C. agreed. "Silver Spoon in Dead Goose. My hat's a sugar brown with a rattler band. Shirt and trousers to match." He waited. "How'll I recognize you?"

"In my hat, straight up, you'll see three turkey tail feathers. And a green necktie. It's the color of money."

# CHAPTER 33

"Papadaddy, are we's lost?"

Behind the wheel of the patrol car, Sheriff Swackert sighed. For several minutes, in the passenger seat to his right, Futrell had been unsuccessfully trying to refold their road map.

"Not likely," said Odessa Bob with patience, privately wondering if they truly were. "Originally we headed *north*. But right now, we have to go *south*, because that's how everyone in Pittman directed us whenever we inquired which way the horses went." Several, O. B. didn't know why, mentioned a strange term: *Jay-Hoo*. A religious sect in black duds.

"What say we forgit about them *horses*," Futrell moaned, "and recover me back my *girl*. Clemsa Lou's run off with a dirty rat somebody, and when I *collar* him . . ." His football fingers messed the map into mayhem.

Instead of driving, Odessa thought he himself ought to be searching the road map for Tickletown, near Dead Goose. But that meant Futrell would have to pilot the vehicle. His stepson manifested equal talent with a car and a revolver. Deputy Swackert's gun holster was still unoccupied.

Back in Chickalookee, at breakfast, Odessa had announced his pursuit plan to Ulivia, including going it solo. His wife convinced him to take Futrell, along with a warning not to come back without her father's livestock, an escaped prisoner (or clown), plus her son's sweetheart.

"Here," Ulivia had insisted, "is Futrell's opportunity to rescue Clemsa Louise and heroically bring her home to her mother. And maybe to matrimony."

After repeated telephoning to Emolly Sue Wetmeadow, Ulivia had extracted that Clemsa had gone visiting her Aunt Harriet up north in Pittman. But today, when Odessa Bob and Futrell paid her a call, no one was at home.

Where was Clemsa Louise Wetmeadow? And with whom?

Add to this, Odessa Bob's main concern, the six hundred and fifty dollars of The Judge's cash, folded once in an envelope bulging a pocket of Sheriff Swackert's official shirt. Money earmarked for Judah St. Jude. Providing.

"Where we going, Papadaddy? I forgot."

"Dead Goose. But first we check out Gnatfly, because that's where all those Pittmanites said the horses were headed. South, to Gnatfly."

An hour later, nobody in Gnatfly had seen or heard of thirteen horses. And whenever Odessa summoned the salt to ask about a religious sect, in black clothing and

146

called Jay-Hoo, the Gnatflyers stared open-mouthed, as though wondering if O. B. had escaped from a mental hospital.

Some almost ran.

The sheriff was about fixing to abandon this goose chase and head for Dead Goose when he and Futrell happened to walk by a barbershop. In its window stood three cardboard signs, permitted by the public-spirited barber, to notify passersby of upcoming local events. One placard heralded a Gnatfly High School performance of *Arsenic and Old Lace*. A second card announced a drum-and-bugle contest.

It was the third sign that slowly captured Sheriff Swackert's attention. And his imagination.

# CHAPTER 34

Dice chattered in her hand.
Not a duet of dice, but a trio of tiny ivory cubes, their birdlet voices chirping to flee her five fingers and fly. Escaping, the dice tumbled across a round tapestry-covered table.

This was no back-alley crap shoot.

It was legend, of luck or ill fortune, brazen, a tale told by ebony pips on six snowy squares of each die. Silent. Stopped dead.

Grandmother Graywolf had been given a timeless talent: the power to read signs and predict futures for travelers who visited Redworm, seeking the wisdom of ancient Egypt. In her parlor they heard the chimes and inhaled the cosmic incense of tranquility. But tonight, Graywolf sat alone. Failing vision forced her to squint in the flickering candlelight. Her toothless mouth gasped in shock.

"Three!" she whispered to the darkness.

Never in her eighty-eight years had she cast three serpent eyes at midnight. An omen? The three dots ordained her to choose only three Tarot cards from the Major Arcana, not a usual spread of ten. Obeying the dice, she allowed the Fatima of Fate to turn three cards faceup.

Fool . . . Chariot . . . Death.

The Fool: A heroic and handsome dreamer of a lad leaving home with a shoulder pole of scant belongings and a dog. Careless boy. A chance-taker, about to fall off a cliff, yet glancing skyward to a sun, defying danger.

The Chariot: A richly robed prince commanding a black horse of evil and a white horse of purity. An epic struggle of shadow versus light. For this charioteer, a choice?

Death: A black knight astride a white horse, a battle charger, wagering his own mortality to joust against danger. Perhaps to discover that death is merely one more adventure.

Now past midnight, and Grandmother Graywolf could not sleep. Forces were advancing upon her: three humans. And many horses. Patiently, she knelt among candles, inhaling the fumes of spice, hearkening to the tinkling tubes of her wind harp. Her soul sought Saturn and a free-flowing ascension. High. Higher. Above all space.

Her spirit touched the face of the young Fool. To her he spoke in song and his walk was a waltz. Yellow boots danced delight. Playing the Fool, he acted as a joker card, a jester. Even as Death threatened, he laughed a lyric of love. Her young Fool dared beyond foolhardy into, once again, more than merely a Fool.

What else? Perhaps . . . a Clown.

# CHAPTER 35

————◆————

Wes Winchester was soaping a saddle.

At his family's small Redworm ranch, standing just outside a tack room and working a soft cloth, he smeared the burnt-cream foam around the pommel horn, across the polished seat, and over the curving crescent of the cantle. A snorting horse caused Wes to shift his attention. A smiling boy, bareback on a black mare, rode slowly as he entered the outskirts of town. Wes squinted. Tullis was ahead of about a dozen odd-looking horses.

"Tullis Yoder," he hooted. "I'll be dehorned."

"Hey there, Wes. How's tricks?"

Cuffing back a stained Stetson, Wes admitted, "Same as always." Seeing the dyed animals, he added, "Yet no trickier than *you*." Wes looked to his left. "That pickup, is that Doctor Platt's . . . with Doc driving?"

Tullis nodded, extending half a hand to shake Wes's. The three fingers felt confident. This boy seemed to have accepted his condition, Wes thought, watching the easy way Tullis slid off the mare.

"Who's with her?"

"The olderly gentleman is her pa."

Studying the color-changed band, Wes asked a quiet question. "Have you and Doctor Platt tripped into the trouble I suspect y'all might be in? I'd appreciate the straight of it, youngster."

Before answering, Tullis milled the horses together, talking to them, touching, until they appeared to settle. Looking at Wes across the back of a bay gelding, the boy swallowed. "Okay, I'll be pie-in-the-face honest. Doc, her pa, and yours truly are horse thiefs. We stole'em, Wes. The Judge and Judah claimed they would put the horses to pasture. But they bended the truth, on account the Threadgill outfit, I'd heard, was fixing to slaughter'em."

Wes sucked a tooth. "A shame. To butcher those beauties while you and the good doctor parade to prison."

"Hope not. I plan to shoulder full blame."

As Wes noticed two people dismount the Ford and head toward him, he said, "That old gent. I believe his name is Hitchborn. If so, he's famous for a flock of felonies. A career con. You can't mean *he's* Doctor Platt's daddy."

"Honest is. And we all might be caught in a heap of trouble, Wes. Can you help?"

It took Wes Winchester only a breath to consider. In his wild bronc days and after one hell of a spill, Doc Platt had pieced a few of his parts together. Be a pity to see her reputation tarnish. Wes figured he owed the woman a good turn.

"Possible. Make that probable. Y'all tarry here for an hour and then, after dark, we'll walk the thirteen into town. In four groups. Together they're plainer than a nose wart. But first, allow me to greet your friends."

Howdys were briefly exchanged.

Wes pointed. "Less'n a mile, there's a dusty-red barn, gray sheds, and a pair of high-rail corrals that belong to my cousin, Ashbel Colpippin. We meet there. But nobody speaks to nobody else. Like we're strangers. Before we go, I'll phone Ash to tell him we're coming and bringing him a band of surprises."

"What's next?" the old gent asked.

"One by each," Wes continued, as he started to collect a few ropes from the tack room, "we bring the horses to Ash, who's horse-hungry for the upcoming Redworm Rodeo. I go first, explain, and then I signal to Mr. Hitchborn and his group. Doc follows. Tullis, you'll lag in tail end. Nobody rides. We all walk."

Evening darkened. Passing out halters and lanyards, Wes assigned specific routes to this odd collection of wranglers.

"A warning," he told them. "Keep to the tree shadows and stay apart. No talk. This ain't a social. Don't try to sell the stock. For the moment we call'em donations."

This was the time to pass out four clean rags.

"What are these for?" Tullis asked.

"To mask your faces. Lucky for us, there's a wind and it's gusting up dust. Again, remain strangers."

With a makeshift bandana over her mouth, Doc Platt spoke up curious. "Wes, why all this furtive, sneaky-pete stuff? We're a hundred miles from Chickalookee."

Wes helped adjust her mask. "Because," he explained, "there's a certain somebody in town that might take a interest in these horses. And in the folks that borrowed them off Judge Hoad."

"Who?" Tullis asked Wes.

"Odessa Bob Swackert."

# CHAPTER 36

Inside the telephone booth, O. B. grinned. There was usual a pulsation of pleasure whenever he was away from Chickalookee and called Mr. Hoad—*collect*. Following several rings, The Judge barked his customary "Heeyo."

"Operator Fourteen," informed a female drawl, "with a person-to-person, long-distance collect call for a Mister Hoad." She continued unhurriedly. "Sheriff Swackert is calling from Redworm, Florida. Do you accept charges?"

"Dang it! I am *Judge* Hoad. Why in thunder is a peace officer calling me *collect*? What's he think I grow here, a money tree?"

"The caller's at a pay phone, Your Honor, and he doesn't have the correct change. Will you accept?"

"All right. Make it brief."

"Go ahead, Sheriff," said Operator 14.

"Judge, it's me. Please tell Ulivia that Futrell and I are stuck in Redworm, but we have captured a culprit."

"You caught Threadgill? Hah!"

"No. He doesn't have the horses. Never has."

"Then y'all nabbed that Hitchborn rat."

"Uh . . . no. But we have detained Mr. Judah St. Jude. Quite by accident, Futrell and I stopped in a Dead Goose diner for eats, and we met Judah with Mr. Threadgill and Sheriff Flowers. We have questioned Mr. St. Jude, yet he seems to know nothing about Mr. Hitchborn's escape, or the whereabouts of your property."

"First things first," Hoad belched. "You wasn't such a dumb dunce as to pay Judah any of my money."

"Not yet. However, there's more. Futrell thinks maybe he spotted our Mr. Hitchborn here at Redworm, in a crowd, and wearing a black shirt."

The Judge fumed. "I don't give all hoot if he's wearing pink panties and roller skates. Hitchborn's a known horse thief who's wanted by most every county in Florida. Get my horses back."

"Mr. Threadgill claims they're *his*. Are they?"

*Wham.* The Judge slapped his desk. "In a pig's rump. Clamp the cuffs on that Hitchborn perp and *whup* him until he 'fesses. Got that?"

Odessa Bob Swackert wasn't intending to whup anyone, certainly not Hitch; yet he'd relish an opportunity of poking the scoundrel with questions.

"Got it," was what he told The Judge.

"O. B., you hang tight to my cash. Don't let a penny of it out of your hands. And never entrust it to Futrell. Hear? I presume you tossed Judah into the slammer, under lock and key."

"As good as. We've confiscated his automobile and

156

warned him he best not leave Redworm until the horse thievery's been solved." O. B. was again smiling. "Oh, another matter. Sheriff Flowers and I have seen Mr. St. Jude wearing an Indian costume, with feathers. Regardless of where the animals turn up, Futrell and I suspect that Judah just might also be the clown."

Hoad's scatological response prompted Operator 14 to pull her plug.

Leaving the telephone booth, Sheriff Swackert's grin drained from his face. He'd heard a cutting edge in Hoad's voice. Vicious and vengeful. Odessa would wager a month's pay that The Judge intended to pay a visit to Redworm, and he made a mental note to call Ulivia. Pronto.

Hoad wouldn't be coming unarmed.

# CHAPTER 37

⸺ ◆ ⸺

Hitch got thirsty. He felt frisky for fun.

It had been two days since his last burning belt of booze, two weeks away from a game of stud poker, and a month without whirligigging a wild woman. How could a man deny so much deviltry and stay decent?

"If I turn any more saintish," Hitch said, sighing, "I might die from strangulation of the halo. Or worse, a dry mouth."

Earlier, upon delivery of the horses to the rodeo corral, Mr. Ashbel Colpippin had tipped Hitch twenty bucks. Be a pity not to rest a foot on a brass rail, lean against a bar, and soothe his thirst with a double shot of dust-cutter. Strolling along the crowded main drag of Redworm, he took notice of the beckoning sign over a saloon entryway.

> # BABE'S
> # GOOD-TIME PARLOR

Five hours later, Hitch was just sober enough to realize he was broke, unable to handle a polka, a pool cue, or a pint. He had fallen down, thrown up, and got brutally whacked on the forearm by a spindle from a busted chair.

A brace of brawny barkeeps—Babe's bouncers—had hurled him out the saloon's rear door and into the trashcanned alley where he now lay. His arm throbbed worse than a hundred hangovers, and he could not stand up or holler for help. Aware that his face was grinding on fragments of broken glass, he wanted to weep.

Inch at a time, Hitch forced himself to belly crawl from the gritty shadows of the alley toward the main streetlights.

People stepped over him. A few stopped to stare, faces he didn't know. Person after person looked, laughed, and left. Until, at last, a kind gentleman hoisted him to his feet. "Your arm's fractured," he said, after gently rolling up Hitch's sleeve to inspect. "It's swollen. Discolored. Where do you go for medical attention?"

"Take me to my daughter."

The man asked, "Is she here in Redworm?"

Hitch was reluctant to answer. The stranger held him up, delicately brushed shards of glass from his face, and walked him to a car. As he fired the engine, the man turned to say, "Where is your daughter?"

Hitch reluctantly said, "At a ranch that belongs to the Winchester family, on Sabal Road. Right nearby. Less'n a mile distant."

"What you really need, old timer, isn't your daughter. It's a doctor."

"Lucky for me, she happens to be one."

159

# CHAPTER 38

"Grip a purchase on him," Doc ordered, "so he doesn't move." How pleasing to have Tullis and Wes Winchester to willingly assist. It was seldom a cinch for one individual to set a fracture on a squirming patient.

Hitch lay on a sturdy kitchen table, mumbling alcoholic apologies with a breath that would nauseate a dead fish. His shirt was stained by crustings of dried vomit.

However, these were not the matters in her mind.

Examining Hitch's arm, Doc's fingertips found the crackling they sought, the internal bubbles. Crepitation. Both bones snapped. Overall, there was swelling yet no internal bleeding. It would be unusual to expect any serious arterial damage. Never without her black-leather medical satchel, Doc produced a small vial that contained five cubic centimeters of liquid procaine, a local anesthetic.

"Occupy him," she told Tullis.

The boy obeyed. Even so, Hitch winced at the two needle jabs of anesthetic but said nothing.

"Procaine," said Doc, "works in about two minutes.

At the most, three. The area becomes completely numb and imperious to pain."

Pulling slowly but firmly, she first aligned the butts of the radius bone, repositioning the segments to knit. As her father's arm wasn't meaty, her fingers felt the bone reuniting into place. Doc did likewise with the lesser ulna bone. She had sent Wes Winchester outside to find a couple of foot-long splints. With a smile of success, he burst through the kitchen door.

"Paint stirs," Wes announced. "Okay?"

"Perfect," said Doc. A stir stick was applied to brace both above and below Hitch's forearm, then bound in place by white, inch-wide surgical tape. One piece, in a continued spiral wrap, wrist to elbow. "There," said Doc. "While he's mending, our beloved bog trotter will be able to bend his wrist at will."

"Best you warn him," Wes mumbled, "that he better not be bending it in a barroom."

"Get him up," Doc instructed Tullis. "Parade him around outside for a spell until his head clears. If ever. Then usher him to the blanket on the porch. He's too aromatic to sleep indoors."

Tullis had vacated the kitchen. Wes handed Doc a clean hand towel as she finished scrubbing her hands at the sink. "Doctor Platt," he said seriously, "there's a situation brewing that you ought to know. I happened to meet Sheriff Swackert in town today. He'll maybe be taking your father into *protective custody*." Wes's tone didn't set comfortable with Doc. His words were a warning that howled like an evil omen.

"Why? Let's have the real reason, Wes."

"Okay. Listen up. Soon an unexpected somebody may be arriving here to Redworm. He don't wear a badge, but he can turn mad-dog mean and bears a grudge. He'll use poker or stole horses as a excuse to harm your daddy."

Doc gasped but said nothing, as it appeared to her that Wes Winchester had more to say.

"O. B. talked to Ulivia, and she warned him this certain individual is probable packing a weapon. Odessa will do his best to head him off, but there are a few obstacles to prevent his doing such. Family problems. It's possible that none of us knows the muscle this man controls. Or the blood money he can spend. Let's hope he's too cheap to spend it."

Without asking, she already knew the name of this individual who would be a threat to her father's safety.

E. Carvul Hoad.

Later, unable to sleep, Doctor Platt stared at a night ceiling. Her main worry wasn't her father, because Hitch was so determined to kill himself. By one madness or another. As for Judge Hoad's animosity, well, he was a tyrant that nobody could reform. Her prime concern was for someone else—and his obsession with winning an 8 buckle. Investing eight seconds of his life or perhaps all of it.

On the back of a bull.

# CHAPTER 39

Early next morning, I was at the arena.
Deep in the right pocket of my raggedy pants, my
hand touched the twenty-dollar bill that Mr. Colpippin
had slipped me for horse delivery. Twenty bucks. Wow!
Felt nifty to be rich. More money than I'd ever toted.
But I was fixing to risk half of it to enter. With the
remaining ten bucks, I'd trade at a proper store to pick
up a few presents for everybody. Except myself. What
little Tullis Yoder needed, he already had. Fun and
friends.

The only trinket I had a yen for was a silvery belt
buckle with a 8.

I laughed. Knowing that I was about to participate in
a real rodeo reminded me of a joke that one of the old
Big Bubb Stampede saddle bums often told:

"You hear about Tex?"
"What about him?"
"A bull tore him to pieces."
"Really? Where's he at?"

"The hospital."

"Yeah, but which room?"

"Oh, he's in twelve, thirteen, and fourteen."

Here at the rodeo place there was a plenty of cow-pokes under smart hats. Stetson felt. Not no bent-up cardboard, like mine. They walked around in polishy footwear, each boot boasting a shiny spur that jingled a rowel wheel at every strut. Before I had to ask, there was a sign.

REGISTER HERE FOR EVENTS

To enlist, I stood on line with waddies who seemed salt-seasoned enough to keep all winter. Hides of burnt leather and wrinkled voices that must've gargled with gravel. After a wait, it come my turn at the counter, where a dent-faced duffer checked me up and down. Couldn't see much of him except head and shoulders.

"What'll it be, cowboy? Choose your coffin."

"Howdy, sir. Can I please enter?"

He smiled with busted teeth. "Okay, sonny. One crutch or two? Do you cotton to buck broncs and limp on one crutch? Or try bulls, for two?"

"Uh . . . I'm a buller."

"It'll cost ya ten smackers a go-at. Cash in advance. On account of a shortage of bucking stock, every cowboy gits only one bull."

"One," I told him. "One's all I need to final stick for

eight and win, if I draw me a devil. Hope you got change for a twenty." My right hand still rested in a pocket.

"So," he said, "you think you're a bully? Do allow me, baby cheeks, to show you a bull rider's hands. Take a gander at my paws."

What he placed on the counter, pointing my way, were no longer human hands. Merely broken bits of scars and bone. Dog-chewed meat. That's when I played my ace. His eyes wided as I flashed a twenty bill in my diminished right.

"Tullis Yoder," I said, spelling both names.

"Guess you paid your dues, son." As he added me to his roster and returned me ten dollars, he warned, "Don't try to grip using that wreck of a claw. Wind the wrap around your lefty. And good luck, kiddo." Reaching out, he grabbed my skinny forearm with his busted-up hand. "Son, if you spill off bloody, walk away tall and quit. Hear me? *Quit*, while you still got a few particles of yourself to glue together."

Swaggering away from the sign-up booth, I attempted a cocky grin in spite of a stomach knot the size of a pumpkin. My nerves needed a change. But to what? I decided to pay call on my beloved four-footers. They weren't too hard to locate.

A wrangler asked why I was hanging around the stock, so I answered him polite: "Watch careful, sir, and you'll see evidence."

Bending to slip through the corral bars, I just stood there, my back to rails, to allow Char to smell me. Turning her handsome head, nostrils flaring, ears tilted forward, she nickered a welcome. Came right to me and placed her head in my arms. I inhaled her entire maredom.

Char followed as I found Stocky, Bay, Goldie, Dapple, and the pinto, War Paint. Although I gave every animal a bear hug, Char nudged them apart from me, forcing the others to savvy that I was her property and belonged only to *her*. Several men stood outside the corral, resting boots on the bottom rail, arms on the upper, observing Char and me.

One remarked between brown spits, "Nothing sweeter than to git owned by a mare. Almost like you're again a boy and found a second mom."

It wasn't easy to leave.

Hunching through the corral slats, I straighted up and bumped smack-dab into somebody. Took the big fellow only a breath to grab the front of my belt in a granite grip. His hold didn't hurt. But certain held. Only then did he warm up a smile and speak in a soft way.

"Well," he said, "if it ain't the Chickalookee clown."

# CHAPTER 40

O. B. maintained his clutch on the boy's belt.
To their left, he eyed a empty bench that stretched half a rod beneath oak shade, appearing to invite a conversation. They sat, a foot apart. The young man's clothing, he noticed, was little more than ratty rags. He doubted there was even one dance left in those pitiful beat-up boots. Yet there was a finery to his nature, a quiet resolve, like a new candle in a rusty lantern.

Releasing his hold on the boy, Odessa Bob said, "You're *not* arrested. Hear? But I'd appreciate you don't skedaddle off. Is that a fair shake?"

"Plenty fair, sir. More'n I got coming."

"Last time our trails crossed, it was at my jailhouse in Chickalookee, where you posed as a deaf-mute. You wouldn't spoke a word if your undies was on fire. Today I heard your palsy palaver with the horses. So gab. Your name is . . . ?"

"Yoder. Tullis Yoder."

"You rascal." O. B. shook a finger at him. "You must a been the clown that Futrell, my deputy, claimed was in a cell with Mr. Hitchborn. True?"

"Yessir."

The boy's eyes squarely met his, strong, steady, his voice never wavering. "You helped to liberate Doc's pa from my facility. Clever. But we have a more serious problem. You, Hitch, and Doc stole the Stampede stock, drovered'em north, and donated same to Mr. Colpippin."

Tullis held a long breath, then let the tension slowly escape. "That's exact the truth of it, Sheriff. You nailed it dead center. But we didn't steal'em for profit."

"Son, I know what y'all done and why." O. B. sighed. "Well, I got a solution if I can convince folks that your larceny is legit. How? By a visit to Mr. Ashbel Colpippin to inform him that he *won't* be arrested for fencing stolen property. He uses the stock for a rodeo, then he pays Judge Hoad out of the gate receipts. Mr. Threadgill never took possession and is totally out of the picture. It's all Hoad."

"But I heard The Judge is more cantankerous than Mr. St. Jude."

Odessa's mouth felt sudden dry. "He can turn ornery. Once he learns that Mr. Colpippin needs the Stampede horses, Judge Hoad'll double his price. Then, if Colpippin can't afford it, the matter closes; but The Judge won't collect a cent."

"Trouble?" the boy asked.

"Lots. If Hoad gits stuck with those thirteen horses, he'll anger and harm somebody. He is already steamed. A further financial loss will torch his temper."

Tullis glanced at his distorted hand. "Doctor Platt

168

has give me a home, Sheriff. She's been righteous caring. So I dasn't let Doc be hurted or shamed. Hitch be the sort to hightail, run off, and never found. Doc ain't cut like that. She'd try to burden all the blame. To protect *me*. Even though the whole shebang was *my* idea."

O. B. agreed. "Possible. That's why I'm talking to you thus. To make you savvy how things stand, and how myself might want to do a mite of mitigating."

"I'll help, Sheriff. Any way I can."

"Good. If things all work out with amity, maybe we'll all stay up here to Redworm, revel a rodeo, and avoid damaging the innocent."

Odessa Bob Swackert was just beginning to feel relieved about the Redworm situation, with a good chance that matters might mend. Even though there were still a few hotheads to cool. Pulling a soft package of Mail Pouch from a back pocket of his uniform trousers, he unrolled, pinched, and stuffed a tobacco wad in his mouth, feeling it nestle between his cheek and gum.

"Am I free to leave?" Tullis asked.

"You be. Just don't skip out of town."

"Thanks. Right now, there's a somebody I'd sort of like to go see. Staying at the General Redworm Hotel. But this person had nothing at all to do with our horse thiefing. She's a proper young lady from Chickalookee who likes horses. Someone I been growing fond of. You might know her people."

"Perhaps. What's their name?"

"Wetmeadow."

O. B. swallowed tobacco.

# CHAPTER 41

Futrell paced the hotel room floor.

Eight feet over and then eight feet back, his size-thirteen cowboy boots stomping to and fro, flushing up the cigar ashes of previous occupants, as well as expressing impatience. And anger. "Has some rotten skunk abducticated my girlfriend?"

Futrell Hoad Swackert was raging for revenge.

On one of their twin beds, his stepfather lay curled up cozy in a afternoon nap. Futrell lightly lifted the car keys from Odessa Bob's pocket. He eyed his own empty holster. Best be armed in a strange town, he thought, particularly during a rodeo week. Folks might rip into rowdy. So, to ensure his being on the safe side of the situation, Futrell also borrowed Papadaddy's six-shot Colt Police Positive .38 Special.

The weight made his hip happy.

He had driven the patrol cruiser less than half a block when, eagerly rounding a corner onto the principal thoroughfare and shopping district, his eyes popped. *There.* Was it? *Yes!* Up ahead, Clemsa Lou was slowly strolling.

But not alone! She was smiling, gazing into the attentive eyes of some lanky, poor-dressed . . .

Feverishly, his boot pressed the gas pedal, and then, in a panic, had to hit the brake. The tires squealed. Too late.

CLUNK. CRUNCH.

"Oh, no!"

He had rear-ended a junk heap of a pickup. Severely. Seconds later, a produce picker got out from the pickup and shook a fist and cussed Mexican at him. Swarms of yellow honeydew melons were bouncing and rolling all over Redworm. The melon man's wife, extremely pregnant, also screamed and pointed. Motorists honked and hollered, and it seemed that every street dog in town began to bark.

Even worse, the impact had activated his patrol car's emergency siren: *Whoop. Whoop. Whoop. Whoop. Whoop . . .*

Rolling down the car's window, Futrell tried to apologize, until the enraged truck driver splattered his face with a ruptured melon. The wife was whacking the cruiser with a rake.

Finally prying himself from the seat, spitting melon seeds, Futrell straightened himself up to full uniformed stature, only to perceive that he was double the dimension of the pickup owner. A blow from the rake knocked the deputy's hat off; a small child retrieved it, then disappeared.

"Clem!" he shouted. "Clemsa Lou, darlin', can you possible hear me? Clemsa! Clemsa Louise?"

Surrounded by the disorderly din of tumult and temper, not to mention multitudes of mashed melons, Futrell couldn't even hear himself. Again he hollered Clemsa Lou's name to no avail, suffocating in crowd noise; honking, barking, cussing, plus his own siren. A bad dream? Was he actual asleep on the other twin bed? Would she leave? How could he attract her attention?

"Ah," he said, "I got it."

Drawing his stepfather's Colt Special from his holster, Futrell fumbled the safety off, aimed it straight up into the sky, pulled the trigger, and fired. Six times.

BAM. BAM. BAM. BAM. BAM. Click.

Only five shots? Then he remembered Odessa Bob usual kept the firing pin opposing a empty chamber.

Women screamed. Strong men fainted. In only minutes, it appeared that almost everyone in Redworm had assembled around him. A small girl even requested that he do it again, until her mother hauled her away. Only then did she wail. Repeatedly, he bellowed Clemsa's name, yet no one could now hear anyone else, and he was totally amid strangers. Not a single familiar face.

Except one.

"Futrell," said Odessa Bob, close enough for the deputy to read his lips, "please do hand me the revolver."

He had to shout to explain. "Papadaddy, the reason I discharged your weapon is because I was mere trying to coax everyone *quiet*."

After checking the Special, closing it without reloading, and then tucking it into his belt, Odessa Bob looked up at him and asked, "How, pray tell, did this ado start?"

"I seen *Clemsa*."

"So, to impress her, you decided to louse up a load of melons, damage two vehicles, spook everyone in Redworm, and crank up a riot."

"Not exact, Papadaddy. I was sort of fixing to . . ."

An overripe melon hit Futrell's head, splattering into green pulp.

"Here's what," his stepfather said. "You are to pay this here melon grower for his truck repair, produce load, and lost time. Two hundred dollars ought to square it."

"I don't carry that much," Futrell said.

"Then please, with a polite bow, give the Mexican gentleman your sincere apology, plus all the cash in your wallet. As of now, your benevolent grandfather, Judge Hoad, is donating two hundred dollars from his horse recovery fund, which you shall explain to The Judge soon's we see him."

"He won't like it, Papadaddy."

"No." Odessa grinned. "Not hardly. Furthermore, you and I will start considering your future occupation, other than being a keeper of the peace."

Eyes closed, Futrell's face melted to a puddle of sorrow. What, he was wondering, would be the next woe to wander his way? Opening his eyes, he flinched. There, before him, stood the only gal for whom he'd ever had a hanker. A very sudden appearance.

"Futrell," said Clemsa Louise, "you big sweet ol' lug nut, *please* stop pursuing me. We aren't going to marry. Not now, and not ever." Her hands found his. "But I'll remain one of your closest friends, if I may, please. Now don't you pout." She touched his face. "Someday, you'll meet a lady who'll bear-hug you to bits. Because you deserve *her*, not me. Hear?"

"Listen to her, son," Odessa Bob said, after turning off the siren, "and give her pretty cheek a gentle kiss good-bye."

Futrell couldn't.

As he watched his pretty Clemsa Louise walk away and into the crowd, all Futrell could do was bite his lip. He wanted to die.

# CHAPTER 42

The Winchester household was asleep.

All I could think about was tomorrow at the Redworm Rodeo. Only a few hours left before I'd effort to bohunker my body on a bull, and try to stay there for eight seconds. Belt buckle, are you mine?

The fearsome fret of it stymied sleep. Pulling on my boots, I crawled off the creaking army cot on Wes Winchester's back stoop. All kinds of critters can stir about at midnight. Yet if one solitary human dares to prowl a footstep in shadow, that's a signal for every dog in Dixie to aim a chin at the moon. To bugle or to bay. From far away, at somebody else's ranch house, a hound howled.

Stepping through the squeaky screen door, I happened to see a pig-snouted bat hanging on a eave. I'd disturbed her. Briefly she tented her black-leather wings to tenderly fold around her only offspring, which was clinging by his teeth to the nerveless, false nipples of her upper chest. Mother and infant settled still to camp under starlight.

In the yard, oak branches, and a choir of cicadas in unison beeped into a ballad and then quieted. Night fell as though undecidedly hunting for a spot to den down.

Not quite a cloudless sky. Above, as I walked toward the north meadow, a three-quarter moon seemed supine against its unknown blanket, hanging as an unlikely lantern, its curved edges fraying to fuzz by our Earth's mist.

As I stood beneath a cherry laurel, my eyes seemed to be drawn toward town, leaving me lonesome for Char. Redworm wasn't much of a walk. A lot less if you dogtrot; twenty minutes later, my arms crept around her black neck, whispering to a twitchy ear.

"Char."

Feeling a velvety nose rubbing against my face, I closed my eyes in order to hold all of her horsehood. Wes always claimed that if you're a gentleman around a horse, the gentleness gits returned to you in full measure.

Again, I let her hear my voice.

"Sorry to disturb you, lady love, but I cotton to dump a dose of palaver on somebody, and you're selected to soak it all up."

Patiently, the mare listened to my worry concerning tomorrow, my hopes of not forfeiting a few fingers of a left hand to match my right. And I shared with her my secret desire to draw a tough bull and maybe win some prize dollars. On points. No way I can properly pay court to Miss Clemsa unless I accouter myself into one decent shirt. I'd been trussed in rags long enough and probable appeared to the public about as fine-fashioned as a wet weather scarecrow. My raggedness looked more fluttery than a flag.

"What mystifies me, Char, is that Miss Clemsa don't give all hoot about my sorrowful clothes. Or that half my hand is wasted."

Being with Clemsa was brighter than sunlight. Or hearing a violin for the very first time. As Char's sweet old head was sagging back into night rest, eyes closing, I said good night and left her.

Back on my bony cot, with a slat annoying my meat-less hip, I studied tomorrow. My future was soon to be riding the broad back of a bodacious beef, and I had to stay on. Stick! For eight seconds. Forcing my eyes to close, I still felt Gutbuster's bucking me to breakage as I recollected what a old waddy named Chigger said about bull riders: "A bulltopper always remembers his first bull. And tries to forget his last." Well, for certain, tomorrow afternoon at the Redworm Rodeo, I'd make the acquaintance of my final bull. Last one. Live or die. But suppose that Tullis Yoder gets lucky and wins a big-time bonus?

Would I quit?

# CHAPTER 43

——◆——

Dinah's Diner, at Saturday morning breakfast, didn't offer even one empty counter stool or a vacant booth.

Business boomed. It wasn't due to gourmet grub, Judah St. Jude was thinking as he spat out a piece of eggshell. He wouldn't be surprised if naked natives came here from a Amazon jungle and ordered Dinah's oatmeal to dip their darts in. Yet the eatery was crowded. Rodeo fans, he mused, would munch a mule.

A sign outside read: DINAH'S . . . WHERE YOU EAT DIRT-CHEAP.

In all of Redworm, this diner had the lowest prices, and Judah was neighborly to busted broke. Earlier, he had considered sneaking out of town but had been severely warned by two sheriffs, Swackert and Flowers, that he must remain. At least until the horse-stealing score had been tallied. Since his steer-horned motorcar was officially impounded, its keys in custody, Judah had no choice but to hang around.

Chewing cold toast, he frowned. Until yesterday, his

temperament had been merely moody. However, upon identifying another visitor who'd just arrived here in Redworm behind the wheel of his show-off blue DeSoto machine, Judah's depression soured to a cold hatred.

Mentioning the man's name knotted his stomach. Elberton Carvul Hoad.

The Judge had cheated, robbed, and crowded Judah into financial ruin. Grabbing all the gravy for his personal profit. Closing the Big Bubb Stampede, keeping the livestock. Every head. And, on top of everything else, Hoad had somehow managed to win the loyalty of Miss Ethel Smertz.

Gladly abandoning the burning odors of the diner, Judah, nibbling a toothpick, headed for the swanky General Redworm Hotel, an establishment he now intended to visit. Without cost.

A few minutes later, Judah St. Jude was loitering in the lobby of the hotel, waiting a chance to settle into one of the more impressive and comfortable easy chairs.

He found one.

Luckily, a former occupant had left a fairly fresh edition of a newspaper, *The Redworm Sentinel*. Once seated, Judah could partially hide behind the opened paper and still observe who was leaving the nearby white-tableclothed dining room.

Upon seeing Ethel departing the dining room on the arm of The Judge, both having stuffed themselves with a bountiful breakfast—without bits of eggshell—Judah St. Jude writhed in his overstuffed chair. Resisting an urge to throttle the turkeyish throat of the skinflint who had fleeced his fortune, Judah watched them enter an elevator. They were the only passengers. After the doors closed, Judah discovered at which floor the elevator stopped.

On a dial, the arrow paused at the numeral three.

Third floor.

Playing the big shot, pretending that he planned to purchase this hotel, to add to the others he owned, Judah sweet-talked a housekeeper who was checking every room and accompanied her along the hall as she knocked on doors.

"Housekeeping," she announced.

From inside room 309, a familiar voice, one that had snapped at him for too many years, cackled a rude reply to the housekeeper. "No. Do it later. Go away."

Judah went away. Informed.

# CHAPTER 44

H itch forced a smile.

The piercing pain of his arm was killing. He was trying to groan silently, sitting beside Agnolia as she steered the Ford pickup on a very short trip to town.

"Whenever you smile like so," he heard his daughter say, "it's a sure-fire sign you're fixing to tinker up trouble. Why won't you explain what's inside that bundle on your lap?"

"A change of clothes. You'll soon see."

"When?" she asked.

"This afternoon. At the rodeo."

"I'm not attending."

"Be a shame not to."

Agnolia grunted. "If you *cared*, you would have reasoned Tullis out of it. Warned him. Had we a lick of sense, we'd throw a rope around his tomfool neck and drag him through the dust. Far away from those infernal four-legged brutes."

She braked for a traffic light.

Easing the vehicle forward, she shifted. Twice. Glancing

181

at him, she remarked, "When I drop you off, best you not breathe on anyone. The stench of your rotgut whiskey extends farther than hot bacon can spit grease." She paused. "I swear, heartaching over my loss of Frank and Hollis is almost more merciful than having you and Tullis to frazzle me."

But perhaps Agnolia would again have no one, by this day's finish. Hitch couldn't speak it aloud. "Here in town," he advised, "please don't go scouting for him. Ain't sound. It'll only shame Tullis in front of the other men. Sap the manhood that he'll be needing for his event."

"No," she said, "I won't hunt him down."

"Good."

"Instead, I'm going to the General Redworm Hotel to see Clemsa and her Aunt Harriet. Later, to meet Wes and discuss a few matters."

"Remember me to Miss Clemsa," he said. "From the little I seen of her, she's a whistler of a gal. I'm glad she favors our boy Tullis."

Doc nodded. "Together, they must be a gust of glee."

He touched her hand. "Take care, Agnolia."

Exiting from the Ford pained his arm. Hitch was determined to convince himself that the busted bone was causing his eyes to water. Yet he knew otherwise. Within him there was an urge to hold her close, to whisper a good-bye. But it was too late. Too many years had been frittered away in jails, pool parlors, poker tables, and back-alley crap games. So many bottles couldn't fill the most hurtful emptiness of all. Watching her drive away, hugging the bundle of clothes, Rubin Leviticus Hitchborn closed his eyes to embrace his disappearing daughter.

Inside the competitors' entrance of the rodeo arena, he found an extremely busy Mr. Ashbel Colpippin. The man recognized him.

"Yes," he said. "My cousin Wes telephone me yesterday, Mr. Hitchborn, concerning your request to being a limited participant in the ring." Ash shook his head. "No. It's too risky for a man your age. Can't allow it."

"Please reconsider, sir."

"I would. But only if you have a close relation who is an entrant in that particular event. Wes didn't mention that you qualify. Do you?"

Hitch nodded. How critical could one more lie be?

"Are you related to one of the bull riders?"

"Yes. Tullis Yoder's my grandson."

"You might get yourself killed, Mr. Hitchborn."

"No chance." Another fib. "I got vast rodeo experience."

"Well, you'll need to get yourself outfitted."

Hitch patted his bundle. "It's right here."

Mr. Colpippin final agreed and pointed him to the changing shed. Hitch was on his way when another obstacle appeared as one more bump in his rocky road.

"Howdy do, Hitch," said O. B.

"Fine. I'm just fine, Sheriff Swackert."

"You won't be for long. E. Carvul Hoad's in town. He probable has concluded that you are the chief cause of his consternation. I got Futrell looking for you, Hitch, to confine you in a cell for your own safety."

"Why?"

"Well, so The Judge don't blow your head off with that temper of his that is behind a loaded scatter. Or rifle." Odessa Bob gripped his arm. "By rights, Hitch, you ought to face felony charges. But that's not the prime reason I'm arresting you."

"Please. Please don't."

"I have to, Hitch. For your protection."

"Hold it. In only a few minutes from now, Judge Hoad won't be able to recognize me." He indicated his bundle. "Trust me, Odessa. Allow me to go yonder into that shed they're calling a dressing room, and you shall be amazed at what comes out."

"No. You'll disappear."

Hitch winked. "But not the way you presume."

"Okay," O. B. agreed with a sigh. "Take five minutes. If'n you cross me, Mr. Hitchborn, you won't cotton to how rough I'll treat you."

Hitch turned to go. But then faced Odessa Bob to say, "'Twas all my idea to steal the horses. Doc and Tullis were victims of my convincing. I'll shoulder the full blame. You know this is the honest truth, O. B., on account I been a horse thief all my life."

"You got five minutes. Git."

Five minutes later, Odessa Bob Swackert's eyes about popped as he saw the change of clothing on his prisoner. Mighty colorful. From drab to dandy, like a hen flowering into a peacock.

"You be right, Hitch. You certain got yourself properly hid. Not even your daughter would recognize you in that getup."

"Or," said Hitch, "E. Carvul Hoad."

# CHAPTER 45

—◆—

We waited for the news.

Surrounding me was a muster of men, rodeo riders, every one anxious to scan the listings that Mr. Ashbel Colpippin was thumbtacking to a vertical corkboard, which was supported by a pair of unpainted posts. I was way in the rear. In front, the listing prompted a variety of disappointed groans, mixed in with whoops of elation.

"Hot spit," a cowboy hooted. "Looky that! I drawed me Widow Maker. Envy me, boys. Eat your ugly gizzards out. My bull's a forty-niner."

With a grin, he whirled his hat. I understood why.

For a ride's total score, bull points add to a rider's points. Both must perform. Fifty is max for a bull that kicks up a tough buck. Fifty for a rider who sticks. But even the most talented rider can't score big if he draws a weak bull. Widow Maker, we all now knew, was ranked extreme high-up rowdy, as a forty-nine pointer.

As I was a Redworm Rodeo newcomer, plus being not so burly as most of the mature bullers, it took me a

186

spell to inch my way through the bulkier bodies to read the posting. My name was dead last.

## Tullis Yoder..........Black Powder (50)

When my fingertip rested underneath my name, a raw-faced cowpoke grabbed a hunk of my shirt and shoulder, twisting me to look at him.

"You . . . *you* be Yoder?"

Nodding, I said, "Yes. Yessir, that's me."

"Why in hell you manage to draw the crankiest critter that every busted through a chute gate?" The jealous cowboy spat tobacco on my boot. "And yank off that dime-store hat when you talkin' at me."

I obeyed. "Yessir. Meant no disrespect."

"Puny punk. That cussed Black Powder's a gonna stomp, gut, gnaw you fer supper, and puke you out. Sonny Boy, I cain't wait to watch you divide and see yer innards redden the dust."

Without another surly word, Raw Face shoved me hard against the board post and wandered away on wicket legs.

In shock, I stood speechless.

"Aw, don't pay no tench to Gorman," another cowboy told me. "He's a insult to the humanity persuasion. Lace Gorman hates hisself worse'n he hates you or his mother." He smiled with teeth both brown and broken. "Beside, he been shirttail drunk since Thursday."

"Guess he's sore I drawed a high pointer."

The man touched a finger to the figure fifty that

followed Black Powder's name. "You certain done. Glance careful, son. That there bull you're fixing to fork is the only fifty on the chart. That's why they saved him for last."

"You ever see him buck?"

"Once," the cowboy said. "At the Point Gatlin Roar last spring. I didn't draw Black Powder, but a buddy of mine did. Holt Spooner. Holt say that animal sweats so heavy that his back's slippery as a wet seed. And buck? Like attempting to sit atop a epileptic fit."

He walked off singing a sad song.

# CHAPTER 46

Outside the main entrance to the Redworm Rodeo arena, an empty Budweiser beer bottle was lying on its side in the sand. Sheriff Theron Flowers was about to retrieve it to dump it in a nearby trash can until T. C. Threadgill kicked it.

"Dang," said T. C., "how I do disdain getting short-changed in a business setup."

"Don't let it curdle your milk, T. C."

"Well, it do. Makes me feel bandy-legged."

They moved slowly through the crowd, searching for section B, finding row W, and unwillingly seating themselves in seats 7 and 8. Too close to the roof and behind a wide support post. "Sorry seats," T. C. complained with a frown. "Courtesy of the owner, Mr. Ashbel Colpippin, and he's another gent I mistrust. Phones me up, orders horses, and then out of the blue—surprise!—Colpippin cancels 'em, claiming he cooked up a cheaper deal."

Flowers said nothing. He had married Martha May, a fine lady whose misfortune was having T. C. Threadgill for an uncle, and Theron was hoping that the old crab would stop his griping. No such luck. T. C. stomped a boot. "Stinks worse'n a beached whale. After one helping of that Judah St. Jackass and hearing him bawl like a baby, I wouldn't be shocked to learn that St. Jude and a certain Mosquito County Justice of the Peace, name of Hoad, had rigged my rooking."

"Possible," said Flowers. "But not confirmed."

"You seen Saint Jackass today?" T. C. asked.

"No, not recent. About an hour ago, I bumped into Odessa Bob and stepson. Neither of them mentioned Judah. However, I saw The Judge and his lady friend leaving the General Redworm Hotel. T. C., if all of us rest are here at the rodeo, where's Judah St. Jude? And what's he up to?"

"Go git curious"

Sheriff Flowers stood. "Think I owe it to the Swamp County taxpayers to find out. If I can, T. C., I'll be bringing you some information."

Leaving the stadium, about to dash for his patrol car, the youthful lawman encountered the older sheriff, the beefy guy from Chickalookee, who lightly grabbed his skinny arm. Then Odessa Bob leaned close to Theron's ear and whispered, "Just a hunch. Check three-oh-nine."

As O. B. continued on his way, Sheriff Flowers became aware that he had been gently, but not unpleasantly, upstaged.

# CHAPTER 47

The arena parade blasted and blared.

As a band boomed out "Dixie," smiling people stood to cheer Old Glory, the Florida flag, and the Confederate Stars and Bars. Horns honked. Horses pranced, chuck wagons rolled through sand and sawdust. Ropes spun circles. Colts fired blanks. Cowboys were wahooing and pretty cowgirls blew kisses. Children were smearing themselves with hot dogs, popcorn, peanuts, cotton candy, and jumping up and down, spilling their root beer and sarsaparilla.

Clemsa Louise Wetmeadow identified several of the thirteen horses that the so-called Lost Tribe of Jehu had lent to Mr. Colpippin.

Last evening, from the General Redworm Hotel room that she and Aunt Harriet shared, Clemsa Louise had telephoned home, to hear a scad of questions from her mother. Clemsa could not fully respond to one prior to another being pressed upon her.

| "Where in heavens are you?" | "Redworm." |
|---|---|
| "Why there of all places?" | "For a rodeo." |
| "Who's hooting all of that rowdy noise?" | "Aunt Harriet." |
| "Has Futrell found you?" | "Yes." |
| "Will he be bringing you home?" | "No." |
| "You *have* come to your senses, haven't you?" | "Totally." |
| "What's Harriet say about your . . . independence?" | "She said, 'Hooray!'" |

This morning at breakfast, Clemsa had updated Aunt Harriet regarding the futility of Futrell's courtship and her mother's social aspirations. How *marvelous* to marry a grandson of Elberton Carvul Hoad? Her mother's idol, Ulivia Swackert, was not controlling *this* little gal's life. Clemsa Louise made it clear that she could handle husband hunting without Ulivia—or Ulivia's father, The Judge.

Now the three women sat in section C. Aunt Harriet and Doctor Platt had not seen one another "since God created bingo," to use their phrase. "Remember the time . . ." frequently began their exchanges. At noon, Clemsa visited the refreshment stand.

Still no sign of either Tullis or Mr. Hitchborn.

Tullis seemed spellbound by Hitch, quoted him, and was totally enchanted by the old adventurer. Clemsa Louise sighed. If only he'd stop loving bulls. Could she ever groom Tullis enough to take him home? Give credit to Futrell. At least he always presented a spit-and-polish image in his deputy uniform. Or in civvies. By comparison, that adorable Tullis Yoder was a rag rug that one might find on the floor of a broom closet.

His name—Tullis—sparked her smile.

Futrell? Well, he was hopelessly Futrellish.

O. B.'s patience with him, Clemsa had observed, was fixing to snap, and Deputy Sheriff Futrell Hoad Swackert was doomed to become Mr. Swackert, private citizen. His only chance for prominence might be as the next Chickalookee High School football coach. Typical of Florida, the town was expanding, eventually to enlarge the school into a busing bedlam of a discipline problem; ergo, Futrell's massive size would propel him to principal. He'd mess up at CHS and probably at a few others, thus winding up as superintendent of Mosquito County schools.

Sadly, his salary would be triple the amount of the dedicated teachers who'd work under him. At his retirement banquet, someone from somewhere would award Futrell an honorary doctorate degree.

He'd be asked to author a book . . .

## THE EMPTY HOLSTER

A GUIDE TO AUTOMATIC PROMOTION
IN THE PUBLIC SCHOOL SYSTEM

**BY**
**DR. F. HOAD SWACKERT**

# CHAPTER 48

O. B. shifted his weight on the hard arena seat. Rodeos were all alike, and this Redworm wingding was just another ho-hummer.

Sheriff Swackert was one individual in a side-by-side quartet including his stepson, Futrell; the boy's grandfather, E. Carvul Hoad; plus The Judge's all-purpose employee, Miss Ethel Smertz. Seated between her boss and Odessa Bob, the lady was pleasantly perfumed. Not overly so, the way some women try to asphyxiate a maggot. Apparently less than enthralled by calf roping, saddle broncs, or barrel racing, Ethel occupied herself by writing reminders in a small notebook.

Odessa Bob peeked.

*Check lien on Haskin property. Second mortgage? Percentage?*

O. B. smiled. Smertz had *smartz*.

He'd wager that Ethel, contract by contract and deed by deed, had secretly set herself up to be financially solvent. She had learned by observing Hoad's failures as well as his successes. Every day spent with The Judge probable augmented her holdings. No doubt it amused her that E. Carvul Hoad didn't have a grip on how Ethel was egging her own nest.

In the arena, a few bulltoppers managed to beat the eight-second buzzer, but not many. Odessa winced as another rider got tossed and took after by a raging humpback Brahma. Woozy, the rider tried to stand. He was saved by a pair of heroic clowns that helped haze the beast toward the exit.

A barrel lay empty on its side.

O. B. watched a brightly costumed clown scurry unevenly to the fallen clown barrel, right it, and try to enter. With only one leg in, he lost balance and tumbled awkwardly to the arena turf. The crowd hooted its laughter. Again he fell. With extreme effort, the frustrated clown finally achieved entry, ducking into the barrel, headfirst and out of sight. When his arm raised to wave a white hanky, the crowd chuckled and enthusiastically applauded the act.

O. B. was stunned speechless; his mouth fell open. He had seen Hitch in a clown's outfit outside the dressing room, yet he had no inkling that the old duffer would dare to enter the ring. As O. B. uttered a feeble, "My God, it's . . . it's Hitchborn," his stepson leaped to his feet, pointed, and bellowed like a bullhorn.

"Papadaddy! Look yonder. It's *him*! I just saw the clown. You know. *The clown!* I swear. It's my clown."

Deputy Futrell Hoad Swackert triggered the loudest and longest laugh of the entire afternoon. O. B.'s gigantic stepson now stood on his seat, towering over a giggling crowd, pointing, yelling that he'd seen a clown. One of several that had been in view for hours.

If there's one thing that tickles the public funny bone, Odessa Bob concluded, it's when a cop in uniform makes an absolute ass of himself.

Futrell was obliging.

# CHAPTER 49

A circle of blue sky.

From inside the barrel, looking up, that was all Rubin Leviticus Hitchborn could see. Still panting from the ordeal of entering the cussed container, Hitch waited, wincing with the throb of two broken arm bones, wondering if he'd have the bowel, seconds from now, to give a final gift to his daughter.

Earlier, when he had seen the bulletin board notifying that Tullis had drawed the toughest bull of all, Hitch realized the boy would be in dire danger.

Shuddering, knees bent, hands above his head gripping the barrel's rim, he listened to the loudspeaker as the MC announced the next contestant, this afternoon's last bulltopper, the only one who meant something to him. And so much more to Agnolia.

"Hear me, folks," came the reverberating roar. "Keep yo eyes on gate number 5. A first-time rider here at the Redworm Rodeo . . . on the brute of a bull y'all been waiting to witness . . . Tullis Yoder . . . on . . . Black Powder!"

# CHAPTER 50

S heriff Theron Flowers knew where to look.

Entering the General Redworm Hotel, removing his hat, he noticed that the lobby was deserted with the exception of two elderly ladies who shared a brocade love seat. All of the other guests were at the rodeo arena. Perfect timing for criminal activity.

Hoad's room, he already knew, was 309. The elevator was in use, so the lanky lawman easily bounded up two flights of stairs.

Moving briskly along a maroon-carpeted third-floor hall, Sheriff Flowers tiptoed past 303, 305, and 307. Slowing, he listened. No sound. Yet as he crept closer, it appeared that 309 wasn't fully latched. A broken lock? Through a narrow door crack, he saw a glossy item of lady's underwear. It was tossed across the room, as though some B-and-E was ransacking a bureau drawer.

Breaking and entering is never neat.

Because the door squeaked as he pushed it open, the burglar turned to confront him. Flowers made an instant ID. No surprise.

An abrupt arm gesture produced a knife in the perp's hand. Not a long blade. About four inches of glistening steel, yet enough to slice a throat with a single swipe. Flowers snatched a thick pillow from the bed, blocking the door. Firmly standing his ground, the lawman smiled.

"It's over, Mr. St. Jude."

"Yeah?"

Theron nodded. "Please place the knife on the bureau and back away, toward the bathroom. Consider yourself arrested. Make the mistake of trying to use that pigsticker, and I'll still take you into custody. With a .38 slug in your belly. Or your nose will be bleeding and your teeth broken."

"You win, sonny."

"Wise decision. Please face the wall. That's right. Now, if you'll be so kind, touch it, lean, and put your other hand behind you."

Once his suspect was cuffed and being marched down the stairs and quietly through the lobby, the two elderly ladies gave them a curious glance. As Sheriff Theron Flowers politely touched the brim of his Stetson, both women smiled. Softer than lavender.

Felt professional, the peace officer was thinking, not to have to draw a weapon in order to execute a pinch.

# CHAPTER 51

Redworm exploded in rodeo roar.

Yet not every ear listened. Alone, having sought shelter from the afternoon's heat, Graywolf sat in a solace of shade.

Indoors, inhaling incense and hearing only the trilling tinkle of a tiny wind harp, the hands of Grandmother Graywolf now held a pair of Tarot cards. How uncanny that these two entities were destined to adhere, to fuse together, and unite.

Once there had been a third card, but this Charioteer had already made his choice, so his face was no longer lit by the light of one candle.

Finally, two cards only. Becoming one.

Earlier, a circus clown had been laughing and pointing, as if taunting the potent powers that are so spiritually stronger than he. Abruptly, without warning his laughter stilled to a solemn silence. Her candle blew out! The day was dominated by darkness.

Twin cards trembled in her frail fingers.

Fool . . . and Death.

# CHAPTER 52

——◆——

Eight seconds.

Only a tick of time in a human life, I thought, winding the braided leather thong around the four fingers of my good hand. My left. Pounding the loops into my palm.

My inside was a battalion of bumblebees. Electric. Yet qualmy from gullet to gut. No! Mustn't run yellow, even though my flesh was firing up a fever. My throat tried and failed to swallow the dry nothing on my tongue. Beneath the fork of my legs, the sweaty black monster rammed the gate boards, crazy to be loose, to fight this foreign fester that straddled his back.

Worry burrowed into me like a leech.

Above, an empty dome of gray sky, the cloak of a ghost. Plus the spirit of an unknown cowpoke whispering that my wrap wasn't purchased proper across the cup of my left hand.

"Take time," a chute tender told me. "Us boys open a gate when *you* want, not when Loudmouth say so."

Boys? His face was badly beat up by bulls and

broncs. On his broken hand there was a faded tattoo, a serpent twining a Jesus cross, plus a heart with MOM trapped in it. One eye twitched without cease as if clog dancing to a calliope in some haunted honky-tonk.

He studied my grip.

"Not too snug," he warned. "So when big blackie gets rid of you, before you spill, you'll able to yank free. Better'n losing a paw."

Holding up my right, I said, "Mister, I been there."

Compared to his raw ratchet voice, mine twanged sort of high up and womany, like I'd never had living smear me with grit. I had tasted aplenty. But now weren't a time to review it.

Doctor Platt had told me that a educated gent named Goethe claimed a man must, first off, trust himself. This, I full intended. There was a hot heaviness between my thighs. But this time, no urine. Nary a drop. The heat was all Black Powder's doing. A furnace fixing to pick a fight. And by dang, I would battle the brute for eight seconds and be Tullis Yoder, bulltopper.

"You ready, kiddo?"

I nodded.

Our gate opened, the hot voltage of a prod pole jabbed the bull's backside, and he come boiling out the chute, like Satan was fixing to quarter him for stew. First buck turned us half a circle. His hoofs dug into dirt. Hind part high. Second jump was taller and twisted as a kite in a windstorm. So I leaned back on his spine, knees bending, my spurless heels digging his withers like I was trying to goad more meanness into his nature.

The arena band was honking "There'll Be a Hot Time in the Old Town Tonight." But a bull rider ain't long on music appreciation.

Not when over a ton of trouble butts your crotch. He spun. And I stuck with him. Around we went, with Black Powder supplying most the work; all I done was go for a joyride. When he fishtailed, I thought my neck might snap and my head roll clear to Chickalookee. My backbone cracked like a whip. Fingers froze to him, fusing to the three lean, leather thongs. As my fist balled tighter, I tried to punch the critter every time he landed. He had a pattern. Always lit front hoofs only, rear end up, so I laid myself back on him, spine against spine, to spread the pressure. Soak the shock.

Strange, but once his massive curly head turned to stare a eye at me for a split second, maybe wondering why he wasn't shucking me off.

Stick. Stick. Stick.

The word whipped out of me with his every trick, lashing a cut across my cheek. My lip was bleeding and I tasted my blood's sickening sweetness.

No buzzer. Must have got busted and nobody bothered to patch the cusser to end my eight seconds. Buzzer? Buzzer? Please go off so I don't die up here.

Noise. More music. Cheers.

On a wild-eyed bay horse, a pickupper galloped to my right leg to loosen a flank strap and then throwed a strong arm across my back. But no buzzer. No! Go 'way. My hand froze. Wouldn't quit. Using my free right fist, what there was of it, I punched away the pickup man from helping me, causing him to cuss. Spitting tobacco juice into my face, he grinned. Then yanked my hand free.

I fell.

A gritty wall of dirt whacked me near senseless. All around, hundreds of distant faces in a big blur. Somehow I staggered to my feet, shaking my head to locate the remains of my brains, hearing something charging at me. Hard and hot. Beneath my wore-out boots the planet was rumbling and roaring. Pitching a fit.

Black Powder knocked me flat.

He hung too much hurt on me to breathe. Only lie there in the manure dust, trying to wipe my eyes clear enough to see where he'd gone. Couldn't see the bull, yet felt the heat of his anger, hearing his grunt. Grunt. Grunt.

Then I saw a welcome sight. A human form wearing lots of flashy colors that I'd seen somewhere before. A clown.

How could it be Chigger Dill?

# CHAPTER 53

D octor Platt gasped.

Witnessing the mindless and purposeless horror, her lungs seemed deprived of air. Neither mind nor speech could function. Aware only of the intense and irregular hammering of her heart.

Out there, both Tullis and her father lay motionless.

Nearby, a threatening black bull was stubbornly reluctant to leave the arena, repeatedly challenging three horsemen, determined to attack a fallen rider and a mangled clown. The comical rainbow-colored circus costume, so familiar to her, was now dominated by a growing cloud of bloodred.

About her, fans had risen to their feet, straining to see. Parents shielded the eyes of their youngsters. Adults as well as children moaned at the sight. Some even cried.

Harriet and Clemsa Louise were clinging to Doc's arms and body, in shock, as though expecting not protection but medical action. Were they suspecting that Doc could abandon her seat, struggle down the many stairs of a rapidly crowding aisle to make her way toward the two casualties? Impossible. There was no order. People reacted by yelling and pushing, bordering on panic. It was all Doctor Platt could do to restrain Clemsa from bolting, out of control, toward the arena where the bull was finally being contained.

Even before Tullis had appeared astride a plunging horned animal, Doc had recognized Chigger Dill's clown costume, of jailbreak fame. Yet was too stunned to speak. An objection no one could have heard over the rowdy rip of rodeo fans.

How could Hitch do it with a broken arm?

Neither Clemsa nor Harriet knew the barrel clown who, moments ago, had been so shatteringly destroyed by a bull. Of the three women, only Agnolia Moriah Platt realized that she had been watching her surprisingly heroic father die. To save a boy's life.

But a second person suddenly sensed the identity of the dead clown.

Compelled to see, apprehensively standing on her seat, holding the hands of both Harriet and Clemsa Lou, Doc could catch scattered glimpses of the center circle. Tullis was not rising to his feet. Yet he moved. Laboriously crawling to where Hitch lay, the boy touched the broken body.

Then cradled the old man in his arms.

# CHAPTER 54

Judge Hoad lusted for revenge.

Minutes ago, when his grandson, Futrell, had ignited himself into a hoot-holler about some ridiculous *clown*, E. Carvul Hoad began positioning the puzzle pieces, adding them up. The total was plainer than a runny nose. When Futrell had jumped up to yell "Clown!" Hoad had also heard O. B. say a name. Clear as a bell.

Every clue pointed to Hitchborn.

His Honor would be cursed if he'd sit silent at this infernal rodeo show while a horde of horse thieves were cavorting around at liberty. Hoad had the urge to leap to his feet, direct an accusing finger at Odessa Bob Swackert, his simpleton of a son-in-law, and bellow "Clown!" in full volume. While he was at it, The Judge would focus likewise at another feeble excuse for a law enforcement officer, Sheriff Theron Flowers, wherever he was. Rip the badge off his epauletted shirt.

That oil-slicky Swamp County cop was in T. C. Threadgill's pocket. They was *kin*! Related by a marriage. Ought to be a law against so cozy a connection.

Hoad conveniently ignored the fact that O. B. had wed his daughter, Ulivia.

This whole sorry business of horse disposal might wind up costing Hoad a substantial sum. Praise goodness, not a cent had gone to St. Jude. Automatically, his hand darted to an inside suit-coat pocket to feel the cash he'd miraculously recovered from his son-in-law. Still there. But short by two hundred dollars. Well, he'd settle that score with O. B. as soon as this horse swindle got solved and Hitchborn tossed in the cooler. At least he'd gotten back most of it. Patting the bundle, The Judge decided that the envelope felt mutilated. Untrustworthy. Besides, it was white and much too conspicuous.

Removing the bills from the envelope, he returned them to his breast pocket, loose and unbound, crumpled the shabby envelope into a ball, and stuffed it beneath his stadium seat.

"Dang all of this dither."

Hoad had been cheated at a poker game, on the Stampede horses, cheated out of cash, and he'd be cursed if he was going to allow that Hitchborn to cheat the courts out of punishment.

The Judge was fuming so furious that he hadn't watched some young cowpoke stick on a black bull for eight seconds. Then, glory be, once the kid jumped down, the bull knocked Hitchborn to the ground and stomped him. But up here in the stands, everyone stood, so The Judge couldn't see zilch. Out yonder, amidst the action, he thought he could make out a clown on the ground, faking it, pretending he'd got bull-gored. Was it real or fake blood? He yelped at Odessa to take action.

"Haul yourself out there on the sand and arrest Hitchborn before that freaking felon gets up and escapes you again. In some other costume."

But the racket had augmented into uproar and neither of these law-enforcing nincompoops with stars on their useless uniforms paid any heed to the orders that The Judge was whooping. Odessa and Futrell did nothing! They made no effort to collar that horse-thieving Hitchborn, heave him in a hoosegow on bread and water, and throw away the key. That dirty dastard had busted out of jail, failed to appear in His Honor's courtroom, and then swiped thirteen head of Hoad's horses. Several of which The Judge was almost positive that he'd seen earlier, in the rodeo parade.

"Nobody's did anything to stop him!" The Judge's temper was trumpeting. "Hitchborn's out there, fixing to sneak another getaway, and nary a single tomfool sheriff is going to nab the sombitch!"

Crowd noise had become so loud, so intensely concerned, that still no one heeded his ranting. Hoad himself could barely hearken his own voice. In his car there was a gun. In all this hubbub, who'd hear the report of a rifle? E. Carvul Hoad would soon have Hitchborn in his sights, squeeze the trigger, and serve justice. Give the goon exactly what he deserves.

"If'n it needs done," he grunted, "do it yourself."

Without a word to Ethel, Futrell, or Odessa Bob, he

vacated his seat, shoved and elbowed into a hodgepodge of humanity, and pressed forward and down toward the ring. Making poor progress through the mass of boorish bystanders, Hoad considered an alternate route, noticing a staircase to his right that no one was using. Across its entrance, a small rectangular sign hung from a slack rope.

```
STAFF ONLY
```

Well, a dumb caution like a sign surely didn't apply to *him*. Certainly not to a *judge*. Ripping away the rope and sign, he started to descend the steep narrow stairs, rudely followed by a few other fans. Some seemed disorderly, possible drunk. Below, a guard appeared. Pinned on his shirt was some sort of official ribbon.

"Old-timer," he told Hoad, "you can't use these stairs."

"*What?*" Hoad screeched. "Who in blazes do you think you're talking to, you ignorant unwashed trash? I happen to be Judge E. Carvul Hoad, so clear out of my way!"

Behind, more people followed, crowding him, causing His Honor to lose both footing and balance. Reeling into a railing, his upper body leaned over it, spilling his loose money. Some rowdy pushed another, who stumbled against him, hard, forcing The Judge over the bright red safety rail, amidst a fluttering shower of cash, and into a holding pen below.

He fell twenty feet.

The impact struck him so severely that he couldn't cry for assistance. Dollars flew at his face. Where were his glasses? His hand groped in the dust for a ten-dollar bill. "This is mine," he moaned. "Mine!" But in an effort to rise, Elberton Carvul Hoad realized that his hip had turned numb. His leg was limp. Broken.

Too late, he saw the advancing bull.

# CHAPTER 55

Pain.

A plenty of hammering hurt that was biting into me from all directions, like being eaten by wolves.

Lying on my back, there was no use hollering for help, because my mouth had no words and my mind was a junk-littered vacant lot. Couldn't see clear. Everything blurred. Fuzzy. Colder than ice. I had a hanker to ask, "Am I now Kicker Zell?"

How could I raise up to check and see if my left hand was missing? Didn't feel one.

Blink. Blink. Blink. My eyesight was clearing but overhead, nothing but a white sky. A ceiling. Where was I? Right now, I didn't care. Voices. Maybe angels. If so, would they sing and make the hurting go away?

Another matter. Plenty more important than I was. My throat felt dry, preventing me from saying that somebody ought to tend the horses and see that they're fed and watered. In my mind, I was drinking along with every one of them. All thirteen of my beauties.

Yet I couldn't gulp anything down.

Dirt. Pieces of dusty dirt in my mouth, sand and sawdust. Arena grit to chew on. Made a slightly crunchy noise between my teeth so that I didn't want to swallow, even though I was thirsty as a fever. So I told the angels.

"Water."

A voice softly spoke, "He's coming to." And what a blessed voice it was, because it belonged to *her* . . . to Doc.

Her hands were examining my rib cage, collarbone, working my knees and toes. My boots were off! Where was they? Would somebody steal my boots? There's no money to buy another pair, not even second-hand used, so I couldn't hire out to do yardy jobs, not without no boots. I began to cry. Not long, on account a hand lifted my head and another let me drink. Water. Water. Cool and clean. More, more, more—until choking made me cough and quit.

"Tullis? Tullis, do you hear?"

"Doc. Never mind me. The horses . . ."

"Yes, child, they're in caring custody. Close by." A hand touched my face. "You're going to mend. If it's the last thing I accomplish, it'll be to piece you together like a puzzle. Healthy and whole." Doc's voiced quieted. "I couldn't save Frank or Hollis, but I shall heal you or give up medicine and be a field picker."

"Hitch," I said. "Hitch?"

In a blur, I saw Doc shake her graying head. "Done for. He's clean gone. At seventy-seven, my father rolled the dice a final time. But at least he chose his game."

Her face hardened into hickory. Strong fingers tightened on my crippled hand. To comfort her, I said, "Doc . . . you've lost too much family."

"Truly have. So promise me."

Bringing her hand closer to my chin, my lips touched her rough knuckles, and I didn't have to speak a word.

Doc heard.

# CHAPTER 56

⊶•⊷

O dessa Bob Swackert took charge.

Redworm wasn't in his county. But there was no finding Sheriff Flowers and several concerns had to be tended. As a seasoned peace officer, O. B. believed that a sensitive situation begged more for peace than for officity.

He assigned Futrell to oversee a dignified transfer of Mr. Hitchborn's mutilated remains to the Redworm morgue. Once there, the Swamp County coroner could pronounce the old harmonica player as DOA.

Dead on arrival.

Ethel Smertz was most helpful, offering to perform a like service for the departed Elberton Carvul Hoad. He'd be kept at the morgue until Sheriff Swackert telephoned Ulivia with the sorry news. As she was next of kin, funeral arrangements would be entirely in her hands. O. B. promised himself to be as supportive as possible. In fact, he ached to return home and embrace his wife. Considering that Ulivia had been sired and raised by that eccentric essobee Hoad, O. B. gave his wife credit for a few virtues. Besides, she was a countess of a catfish cook.

Tullis Yoder was already in a doctor's hands. Doctor Platt, who was ably aided by Miss Clemsa Louise Wetmeadow and her charming Aunt Harriet.

For a final time, the rodeo band played "Dixie."

Sheriff Swackert stopped to listen, knowing he could appreciate that sprightly old tune a hundred renditions more and always be stirred with pride. It had a way of blending heart to home.

Two men showed. One of them was Wes Winchester.

The other, Sheriff Theron Flowers, informed O. B. of the breaking and entering at the General Redworm Hotel. At present, Judah St. Jude was a guest of the Redworm Correctional Facility, booked for breaking, entering, and assault with a deadly weapon. The knife would be Exhibit A.

Judah was insisting that his name was Chief Panther Bear. So Theron requested that Sheriff Swackert stop in, please, to support a positive ID.

Wes also offered, with pleasure.

Things were quieter now. Rodeo fans had dispersed and every grandstand seat was vacant. What persisted was an aroma of animals, large ones, plus an aura of death. Two deaths. It made Sheriff Swackert recall the Book of Revelation in the Holy Bible, "And I saw, and behold, a pale horse: and he that sat upon him, his name was Death." A pair of feisty seniors who disdained one another had perished here, violently, only minutes apart. Both killed by a bull named Black Powder.

The tired trio of men rested their bodies and their boots in section A, lit up a Camel or cut a chaw, and remained respectful tacit.

"It's not quite over," Sheriff Flowers reminded.

O. B. glanced his way. "S'pose you are referring to our minor misery of illegal horse activity."

"I am. According to my book *Compiled General Law*, section 7356, six months imprisonment or a hundred-dollar fine 'if you pen or transport another's domestic animal to obtain personal benefit. Or for purposes of annoyance or profit.'"

"You memorize it?" O. B. asked.

"Photographic mind." Theron had to laugh. "Not hardly. Since T. C. Threadgill has been warpathing, I made a point to read and reread it, hoping to keep *him* out of trouble. Don't guess your three Chickalookee do-gooders purloined the ponies for personal profit."

"No way," Wes quickly cut in. "My cousin Mr. Ashbel Colpippin will attest to that, and is willing to compensate Judge Hoad, or rather his estate, via Miss Smertz."

"Cancel personal gain," Theron agreed. "What's left is 'for purposes of annoyance.' Offhand, would you wager, Odessa, that ol' Judge Hoad was slightly annoyed?"

The three men laughed humorlessly.

"Incidentally," O. B. asked, "where did T. C. disappear to?"

"His room at the General," said Flowers. "Tuckered out from fussing over naught. The horses weren't his.

217

Not a penny out of pocket, except some hay that was trucked down to Chickalookee. Mr. Threadgill doesn't have a legitimate gripe. By tomorrow, however, he'll be wailing again when he once more knows that no longer does he have E. Carvul Hoad to badger. He might also be tweaked to realize that there being no signed document of transfer, the horses in question still are a part of the Hoad estate."

They crushed out their smokes.

"Say," said Odessa, "speaking of horses, let's us three take a stroll down to the corral. A few personalities, Theron, you deserve to acquaint."

"Can do."

There were several corrals. After a moment's consideration, O. B. indicated a pen holding thirteen. "Wes," he said, "you're our expert on former Big Bubb Stampede stock. Any animals look familiar?"

Wes nodded. "Coats have been tampered with, altered, probable by Mr. Hitchborn, who is reputed to be a pro in such sordidity. Or was. But these are the missing. For sure." He paused. "For that Tullis Yoder kid, or so he called hisself—a boy with a cripple hand, no folks—this band was his family. Named'em all. Lingered to love each and every. Even when he was dog-tired from Judah's overworking him and underfeeding him." Wes spat. "So he whisked'em away from becoming pet food."

Sheriff Flowers sighed.

"Maybe," he said, "you scoundrels are in cahoots to convince me not to collar anyone." He rested a friendly hand on Odessa's shoulder. "You have, sir. No cause of action. Let's break up the party so I can escort T. C. home to Fort Dee, and you can chaperone everyone back to Chickalookee."

Wes smiled. "I got news, gentlemen," he said. "A few minutes ago I met Miss Ethel Smertz. Told her it wasn't the time or place, but I'd be interested in that Big Bubb property for a first-class horse show. She agreed, saying she might be looking for a partner and to bring back the thirteen."

"You mean it?" Odessa Bob asked Wes.

"Honest do. What's sweeter, soon as Doctor Platt reassembles his parts, I got me a special boy in mind for a horse wrangler. I'll notify young Yoder that the job is his'n. Providing."

"Providing what?"

"That he keeps his arse off beef."

Wes left, saying that he again wanted to confer with Ethel Smertz if he planned to be the master of ceremonies at a new enterprise. The two lawmen watched him hurrying off.

Theron asked, "You suppose our dashing Wes is sweet on Ethel?"

Odessa Bob smiled. "Well, they've sure knowed one another for many a year, in Chickalookee. And worked very smoothly together. In the surprise department, after today, not much'll jump me out of my drawers." He chuckled. "And it's none of my business if Wes and Ethel got a notion to get hitched and jump out of theirs."

"Odessa," said Theron, "you *do* have a knack for

forgiving everything, and everybody, to untangle a tempest. How do you manage to juggle so many jelly beans in the air?"

"Son, forgiveness is sort of like Georgia trout fishing—all in the wrist. By the way, as a neighborly gesture, I am inviting you personal to drive down to little ol' Mosquito County for a social visit. Ulivia and I shall entertain you and your spouse for supper. Might prove fun, and also fetch you some professional acumen."

"In what way?"

"Because I'm teaching a one-day course on old-fashioned law enforcement. And you'll be my guest of honor."

Theron respectfully smiled. "Sir, I'll be there."

Sheriff Swackert was alone at last, walking out onto the arena, scuffing the dirt where so much had happened on this dreary day. He glanced at the holding pen where a memorable Justice of the Peace had met a bull. And thereby met his end. Where he was standing, a ratty old scamp of a man had sacrificed himself in a clown suit. O. B. wondered if he could every play a violin again. Not soon. No more duets.

"Hitch," he said, "I shall miss you, ol' heller. Because inside, Rubin, you proved a mite more'n a horse thief."

# CHAPTER 57

The twin green rocking chairs on Doctor Platt's veranda were occupied and activated. One by Doc, the other by a most precious patient.

She sighed deeply.

"Feels so grand to be home." Bending, she loosened an unstylish yet sensible shoe, easing it from a throbbing foot. Then its mate. "Home," she echoed softly, "is about the only place where one can take both shoes and Sundays off." Turning to Tullis, she asked, "How's that pile of pernicious pain you call a person?"

Moaning, as if in agony, he didn't garner a gram of concern from Agnolia Moriah Platt. Nary a nit. He deserved his dose of dolor.

"You are wasting your wails on this woman. I've no commiseration for a chucklehead. When it comes to *you*, Face Powder—or whatever his name is—and I are on the same side of the fence. Had I his hoofs I'd prance on you proper."

"You're still sore?"

"Bet I be." Doc rocked her chair harder and faster to

display her displeasure. "When I review these last days, and the grief you've put me through, I ought to chop you to mincemeat and throw your scraps to the hawgs. The sole reason I regret Hitch's death is because now I can no longer whack that sinner with a broom until he's black, blue, and blighted."

"Well, I have to admit one thing in your favor, Doctor Platt. You certain have perfected a neutral nature."

Doc observed how Tullis had sudden turned his head away from her, so she wouldn't catch his grin.

"Soon as your stitches come out and your fractures have knitted, I've half a mind to kick you out the door, point your sorry self down the dusty road, and holler good riddance until you're finally out of sight."

Tullis stopped rocking. "My, my," he said, "but you do trump up a temper, Doc. Right now, you're boiling like a brisket."

"Temper? Ha!" Doc stamped a shoeless foot. "You've yet to fire my short fuse. All I show people is my cherubic charm and charity. Luckily, you have not seen how I can shift gears from grace to grizzly. But you surely shall, if you ever break your promise to quit bulling forever."

Doc heard a car engine.

Along rolled a Mosquito County sheriff's patrol vehicle and, when it stopped, out popped Deputy Futrell Hoad Swackert. He seemed happy, even though his holster was still empty. "Evening, Doctor Platt. Hey there, Tullis. I hear you received a cash bonus and a honorary belt buckle from the Redworm Rodeo. Good go. Hope you heal up after that tumble you took. How you keeping?"

"I'll glue. Thanks for asking, Futrell."

Fishing a finger into a breast pocket of his neatly pressed uniform, the deputy withdrew two items that he presented to Doc. "Here," he said. "Plumb forgot to give you these. It's your daddy's harmonica. I thought you might cotton it for a keepsake. And there's this faded photograph, a pitcher of a lady trick rider. Her name's to the back."

Doc, without her glasses, squinted at the penmanship.

*Miss Faye Blackstone*
*America's Cowgirl Sweetheart*

Hitch had never once written her a letter, so she could only assume the irregular scrawl belonged to her father.

"Thank you, Deputy."

"Pardon the dent in the harmonica organ," Futrell said. "Y'all probable guess I done it, but I didn't. Honest."

"No one will blame you, Futrell," she said. "Oh, and also please thank the Sheriff for me. Odessa is a loyal friend. A true gentleman, and you are blessed to bear the name of Swackert."

"Thank you, ma'am. I'll say a hey to him. Oh, before I go there's some nifty news to share."

"Really?"

With a shy grin, Futrell nodded. "Found myself a new gal friend, and she's pretty as a peach pie. Wes introduced us. She lives here in Chickalookee and rides a horse like she was born aboard one. She's trying to teach me how to ride. But I keep falling off."

"Congratulations," said Doc Platt. "Her name?"

"Thalia June Soobernaw."

Later that evening, after her beloved Tullis had walked to his bed, on crutches, yet unassisted and strengthening with every wincing step, Agnolia sat alone. Except for a street lamp, her veranda was dark. She closed her eyes, listening to a choir of bugs humming a hymn.

Also hearing a dented harmonica.

# Epilogue

A year had blown by. In a blink.

It was now 1939. A few Floridians planned to north it to New York City and take a gander at the World's Fair, its Trylon and Perisphere at a place actual called—you won't believe this—Flushing.

Here to home in Chickalookee, however, local folks couldn't wait for a grand opening of our Wild Wes Winchester Horse Hoedown. And when it did open, it was a smasheroo! Spanking new, fresh, and white-washed. No bulls. No longer the Judah St. Jude child-labor freak show. But it featured a sentimental souvenir of yesterday that I suggested: a cast-iron, life-size like-ness of America's Biggest Cowboy, a tribute to the memory of a misunderstood man called Big Bubb, whose righteous name was Mr. Nilbut Hoare. Below his statue a bronze plaque saluted his fame.

Children remembered him and brought flowers.

Wes, of course, was still our shining star, dressed like Buffalo Bill and looking horseback handsome, doing his talented trick shots with twin Colts. He was our real headliner. Yet, behind the scenes, our Wild Wes Winchester Horse Hoedown was owned and operated by three able women.

Finances were handled by Ethel Smertz, now also on the board of directors for the Chickalookee National Bank.

Design and decor were Ulivia Swackert's specialities; one had to admit the place was posh and polish. A park, people called it, rife with greenery and blossoms, furnishing the best of food and beverages. No alcohol. Plus invitingly clean seats to eat at. In shade.

Our publicity director was Miss Clemsa Louise Wetmeadow, whose magnetic manner attracted newspaper and radio reporters to view the Hoedown and to broadcast that we were *open,* slightly honky-tonk, yet a frolic of fun.

I was the horse wrangler.

Yet during every show, Wes introduced me as "Tullis Yoder, last year's hero and a Redworm Rodeo Bull-Riding Champion. The first and only man to stick a full eight seconds atop one of Florida's most ornery, Black Powder."

The mention of that bull's name got more applause than did mine, but so what. Being a ham, I bowed, waved, and showed kids my silver belt buckle with a 8 on it.

Wes always added, "Tullis has raised his right hand, placed his left solemnly on a crutch, and swore a oath to his dear ones, promising to never again fork another bull."

I accepted retirement. Also retired my crutches.

Our show's finale was some memorable. As folks

would stand up to leave, the music would suddenly be cut. Merely silence. Then all of our horses would enter with no riders, no saddles or bridles, and would prance around the arena in the pure pleasure of just being a horse. Everyone in the stands stood still, wordlessly watching as if witnessing a quiet bequest from Mother Nature.

A good life. The Hoe, as Clem and I privately called it, proved to be more than a show and became a family reunion in a number of pleasant ways.

A truly missed clown reappeared to rejoin our organization, in the form of Chigger Dill. No more barrel bruises in the ring. Instead, wearing a fresh new costume, he painted clown faces on children and blew balloons into comical critters.

For music, thanks to Wes, Ruby Red and her Saddle Tramps again performed. No longer brass. Instead, a fiddle sawyer, mandolin, guitar, harmonica, and a gal who could slap a stand-up bass fiddle. Our new Hoedown also included a minstrel show and a red-hot all-banjo band to provide spirited tunes, like "Cotton Babes," for a genuine cakewalk. Bones, spoons, tambourines, and a guy with thimbles on his fingers who played a washboard. He could also hambone. Hats and canes and hyuk-hyuk humor. A crib of country corn.

For a good-luck charm, I still kept the little pine wing Clemsa Louise give me off a cone. What's more, I can hold it like a pick, to practice, using my left hand to finger my banjo strings. Already I could play "Alabamy Bound."

Bix Bucko failed to show up because he was in a Georgia jail, a fact that didn't disappoint me, Ruby, or Thalia June Soobernaw, who was assisting Wes's act and flirting Futrell. The former Deputy Swackert was now outfitted in cowboy duds, serving as our smiling security guard. Without weaponry. Futrell's size proved ponderous enough to establish order.

Being a horse wrangler was the coziest job a man like myself ever dreamed of holding. Especially when my coworker, whenever she could spare a day, was Miss Clemsa. So many times, we'd lean against the opposite flanks of a horse, look across his back, and join hands. Inhaling animal fragrance. Clem and I could merely look at each other and touch eyes.

We didn't mention marriage. Too early. The bud of a rose ought to unfold at its own leisurely pace. For one thing, I wanted no children.

Nor did Clemsa. It was a plateful plenty to tend Straw, Stocky, Clyde, Dapple, Sunday, Bay, War Paint, Signature, Goldie, Ghost, Albany, Buck, and my motherly mare, Char. My thirteen charges were a handful. We needed no babies to raise.

However, a child did come along.

For weeks, I'd noticed his hanging around, squeezing between the corral bars to fondle a horse and softly stroke it with a little brown hand. Took him to be Tex-Mex, a half Mexican. I brung him a vanilla ice cream cone, a double dip, learning, as he licked it, that he guessed he was nine, looked six, and strutted a streetwise sixteen. On the subject of job experience, he claimed that he could crawl under a automobile to check for grease leaks. His starved body and stained appearance proved such occupation.

Called himself Car, short for Car Wash.

The only name he owned.

No parents and no home. A dusky speckle of life, stuck on the gummy bottom of humanity's heavy boot. Once I had Wes's nod of approval, I hired Car, telling him he could bed down on a pile of horse blankets in our tack room. For now.

But when he lit up a Lucky Strike, to show off, I tore the weeds and matches from him, warning Car that our deal's off if I caught him smoking anywhere near the property. Smoking and hay are a danger combination. I told him, if guilty, I'd blister his butt until his eyes turned blue. Car understood. Quit the habit like a homesick nun.

During the past year, thanks to the assistance of both Doc and Clemsa Louise, I learned to write with a three-fingered hand and to read a lot. So why not share the luck with my little sidekick?

"Can you write your name?" I asked Car.

He couldn't.

Kneeling, using my fingertip on sand, I printed C-A-R. "There, that's a auto," I said. "For a good ol' buddy like you, let's add a letter." And I stretched it to CARL, which his slow smile seemed to sanction. "You could also do with a second. A family name."

"What you?"

"Yoder."

"That'll do me fine. Can I be Carl Yoder?"

"It'd be a honor."

His teeth beamed me a grin.

Char somehow sensed that Carl belonged with me as much as my smell and accepted this horse-chestnut-colored colt as *hers*. Devotedly, she stood close to a particular water trough so Carl could climb to her back, his gritty, pink-soled feet hanging by each flank. She paraded him with pride. When tired, Char returned to the trough so he'd safely dismount.

And kiss her muzzle.

Clem and I presented Carl Yoder to Doctor Agnolia Platt, whose initial suggestion was that he required a bath. And de-louse shampoo. It took the strength of three of us. In frustration, a few dirty words got spoken, not all of them by Carl, but the bathing bout completed. He shined like a wet pebble.

Food was next. My boy behaved better, ravenously wolfing the goodies that Doc piled on his plate. Then we all took an evening stroll. For some reason, in the direction of a horse corral.

I hoisted Carl to where he was happiest, on Char's receptive back, but my mare refused to budge. This dowager's day was over, Char knew, and perhaps wondered why four humans couldn't savvy the simple significance of a sunset.

"So," sighed Doc, "he is now a Yoder."

I paternally nodded.

"How inviting," said Clem, giving my hand a secret squeeze. "I foresee that Carl won't be the only person

230

who hankers to become one."

My hand agreed with hers.

To the west, a sleepy Florida sky blossomed to grace us with a garden of cloud petals. Beneath the moss-hung Southern stillness, standing between Doc and Clemsa Lou, their fingers woven into mine, I grew a hair taller to manhood. A nickering nudge from Char, plus a soft smile from her very young and freshly bathed buckaroo, blessed us a benediction.

Our sundown was dreaming of a dawn.

Faye Blackstone, whose picture Hitch carried in his shirt pocket, is a real person. A champion rodeo trick rider during the 1930s, she is a member of the Rodeo Hall of Fame.

FAYE BLACKSTONE DURING HER HEYDAY

A SMALL AMOUNT OF AIR
THAT ISN'T THERE

A Flat           "DUMPTY'S DEFINITIONS"

First U.S. Edition

First published in Great Britain in 1995 by William Heinemann Ltd., an imprint of Reed
Consumer Books Ltd., Michelin House, 81 Fulham Road, London SW3 6RB, and Auckland,
Melbourne, Singapore, and Toronto

ISBN: 0-316-60202-7
Library of Congress Catalog Card Number 95-75601

10 9 8 7 6 5 4 3 2 1

Consulting Designer: Douglas Martin    Paper Engineer: David Hawcock
Produced by Mandarin Offset    Printed and bound in Singapore

Once upon a summer's morning,
The Jolly Postman woke up yawning,
Cooked his breakfast, fed the dog,
Read the paper, kissed the frog,*

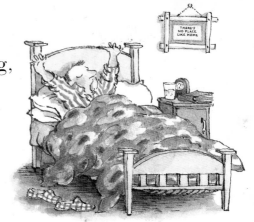

Got his coat and grabbed his hat,
Found his tire was pancake flat,
"Blow me down!" (Blow me up!),
Went back for another cup,

Rubbed his chin, scratched his head . . .
And *walked* to work instead.

*Only joking

A letter for the miller,
A postcard for the mice,
A parcel for the pussycat,
A pair of boots—that's nice!
A letter for a long-haired girl
A letter for a shoe!
A phone bill for a rowboat,
But, goodness—where's the crew?

The Jolly Postman takes his ease,
A shady spot, a cool breeze.
Till, suddenly—Oh, dear! Oh, my!—
A *giant rattle* from the sky
Gives him a tremendous clout . . .
And knocks him out.

Meanwhile, above, a giant mother
Says, "Never mind, we'll buy another."

The tire was flat, the Postman's flatter;
His poor dog wonders what's the matter.
He licks his master's pale cheek.
The Postman seems about to speak.
"I'll be all right—I'm feeling better."
And then a rabbit with a *letter*
Goes running by; the dog gives chase.
The Postman, too, joins in the race.
All three of them—well, bless my soul—
Go diving down a rabbit hole.

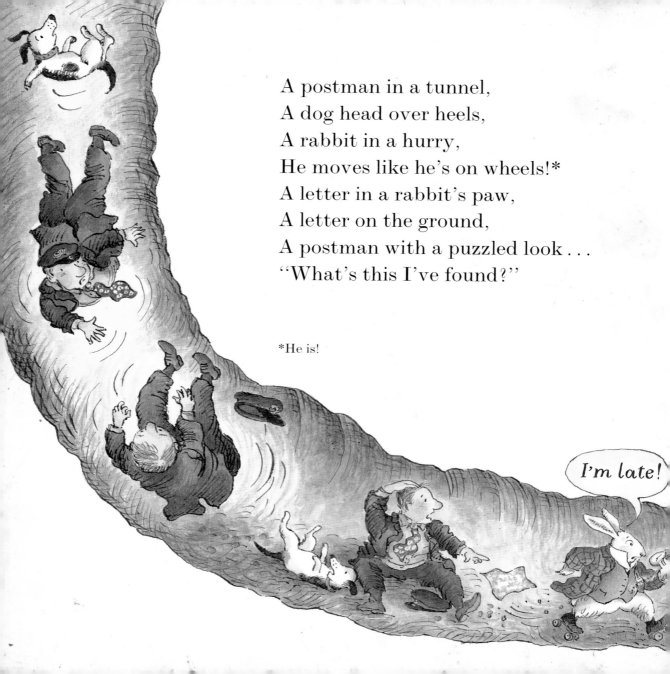

A postman in a tunnel,
A dog head over heels,
A rabbit in a hurry,
He moves like he's on wheels!*
A letter in a rabbit's paw,
A letter on the ground,
A postman with a puzzled look . . .
"What's this I've found?"

*He is!

I'm late!

And now—hurray!—the Postman sees
A table set beneath the trees,
A girl (named Alice) in a chair,
A Hatter and a Mad March Hare.
"Good-bye! Hello there! Lovely weather!"
The Hare and Hatter shout together.
While Alice says, "Here, sit by me.
How are you? Would you like some tea?"

The Postman sips, the Postman drinks.
      The Postman shivers . . . smiles
            . . . and *shrinks*.

What will he do?
How will he cope?
He's shut up
Like a
tele-
scope!*

*And his dog, too.

"My word!" the Pocket Postman cries,
Astonished by his pocket size,
His pocket dog, his pocket hat.
"What kind of cup of tea was that?"

With tiny steps in tiny shoes,
He travels on in search of clues
And finds, quite soon, a curious tree
Of letters. "Is there one for me?"

Alice, meanwhile, now twelve feet tall,
Has made a face
        and begun to bawl.
She ate the little EAT ME cake:
A *huge* mistake.

Feeling better, flying high,
The Postman waves the bat bye-bye,
Thanks the pilot—"First-class flight!"—
Bails out at a dizzy height,
And lands with a bump on a cookie tin.
"Is anyone in?"

Meanwhile, a *wolf* in postman's clothes
(How did he get them? Goodness knows.)
Arrives to offer bad advice.
(Shut your eyes, this part's not nice.)
"EAT ME? DRINK ME?—that won't do.
This'll solve it: I'll eat you!"

"No fear!" the Postman cries. "You scamp!"
And climbs into the nearest . . . stamp.

A flabbergasted postman,
A scary spidergram,
A postman in a pickle,
A postman in a jam.
But now, look out,
There's worse to come.
Don't stop—Keep going—
Scram!

A bat, a rat, three newts, a frog
Pursue the Postman and his dog.
"Is this a dream or am I mad?"
Then, just when things look *really* bad,
The Postman's cries for help are heard
By a friendly passing *postal* bird.

Blow me down! Blow my nose!
Man in daisy; dog in rose.
Meanwhile, above them in the sky,
A *flying* letter flutters by.
Without a name and no address;
For whom is it intended? Guess.

Away from the house and down the lane,
The Peppered Postman racks his brain.
As he worries more about being less,
He meets a girl in a gingham dress,
A scarecrow, a lion and a tall tin man,
Who offer to help him all they can.
"You must come with us," they cry, "because . . .
WE'RE OFF TO SEE THE WIZARD OF OZ!"

Then, just when the Postman's about to agree,
He's blown away by sneeze number three.

ATISHOO!

A postman with a sparkling map;
A girl (named Dorothy).
"This is the place we told you of—
The road to Oz!" says she.

A postman with a tiny frown;
A tiny dog, so small,
You almost need a microscope*
To know he's there at all.

*Or a lens

Meanwhile, a girl
so hugely high
You'd need a *telescope*
to spy
If she had washed
her neck or ears,
Above the "tiny" trees
appears.

"It's only me,
for goodness sake;
All I did was eat a
cake.
Then I shot up like
a rocket!"
She has the Hatter
in her pocket.

*Alice, of course

And now—almost—the final scene:
Down in the clover, cool and green,
The puzzled Postman rubs his chin
And wonders, "How did this begin?"
Suddenly—Oh, dear! Oh, my!—
The *Gingerbread Boy* comes hurtling by;
Avoids with ease the Hatter's hat,
But knocks the Jolly Postman . . . *FLAT.*

A curious rippling in the air,
A ringing in the ears.
The scene begins to shift and fade
Until . . . it disappears.

CURIOSER
AND
CURIOSER

A postman, much to his surprise,
Returned now to his former size.
Things are not always what they seem.
Was all that shrinking just a dream?

A miller with a cup of tea.
"You've had a nasty bump," says he.

Once upon a summer's morning,
The Jolly Postman wakes up yawning,
With a bandage round his head
And a crowd around his bed,
And a dog curled up upon it,
And a baby in a bonnet;
A bottle and a spoon:
Three times daily—get well soon.

And the nurse says, "Feeling better?
Look, the postman's brought a letter!"*

*Post*woman*, actually

The Jolly Postman reads his book
With, once more, a puzzled look,
Eats his breakfast on a tray,
Gets up later in the day,
Takes his medicine, takes a stroll,
Sees a gander score a goal,*
Eats his supper—cheese and bread—
Reads his book again in bed,
Snuggles down—a cozy spot—
And starts to dream . . . or maybe not.

*Not joking!

Meanwhile, from a tremendous height,
Out in the dark and starry night,
Above the hills and under the sky,
Where warm winds blow and witches fly,
Head over heels and golden brown,
A giant . . . *teddy* tumbles down.

The End (really)